Mom tur

right behind her. We park ourselves

refrigerator.

"I bought a new carton on Thursday," she says, twisting her opal ring around and around on her pinkie. "I haven't used any eggs at all. If you haven't either, there should still be a full dozen."

"I haven't used any," I tell her.

She takes a deep breath and tugs open the refrigerator door. She has the grim demeanor of a fourteenth-century villager about to open a vampire's coffin. She takes out the egg carton and places it on the counter. Gingerly, she lifts the lid.

There are four eggs inside, crowded together at the left end of the carton. The rest of the carton looks starkly empty, like eight tiny bird's nests emptied of occupants.

"Oh!" Mom clamps a hand over her mouth. "How can this be?"

I can only stare at the carton in silence, dazed by the undeniable truth. Somebody is taking our eggs and using them to attack mall stores. I just don't know who or how or why.

Mall Girl Meets the Shadow Vandal

by

Kimberly Baer

This is a work of fiction. Names, characters, places, and incidents are either the product of the author's imagination or are used fictitiously, and any resemblance to actual persons living or dead, business establishments, events, or locales, is entirely coincidental.

Mall Girl Meets the Shadow Vandal

COPYRIGHT © 2021 by Kimberly Baer

All rights reserved. No part of this book may be used or reproduced in any manner whatsoever without written permission of the author or The Wild Rose Press, Inc. except in the case of brief quotations embodied in critical articles or reviews.
Contact Information: info@thewildrosepress.com

Cover Art by *Diana Carlile*

The Wild Rose Press, Inc.
PO Box 708
Adams Basin, NY 14410-0708
Visit us at www.thewildrosepress.com

Publishing History
First Edition, 2021
Trade Paperback ISBN 978-1-5092-3512-4
Digital ISBN 978-1-5092-3513-1

Published in the United States of America

Dedication

For Coleen—my childhood best bud,
my grown-up gal pal, my forever friend

Acknowledgments

Writing and publishing a book is a team effort. Thanks to the following people, who were instrumental in helping to usher *Mall Girl* into the world:

My children—Tiffany, Derek, and Ryan—for believing their mom could be a writer and because the books they shared with me while growing up spurred my interest in middle-grade fiction.

My sweetie, Clint Chadbourne, for his unflagging support and encouragement.

Tiffany "T. J." Baer, Clint Chadbourne, Bill Chadbourne, and Coleen Martin, whose careful readings and thoughtful feedback vastly improved the story.

My "Invisible Ink" pals and fellow writers, Phillip Thompson, Jeff Bishop, and Jason Kraus. They thought we were just goofing around on that fateful day, but their witty comments inspired the book's title.

Dianne Rich, editor extraordinaire, whose eagle eye and sense of logic made this story the best it could be.

Talented cover artist Diana Carlile, for bringing the essence of the story to life graphically.

All the other talented folks at The Wild Rose Press for the care, enthusiasm, and professionalism they apply every day while shepherding each book along on its publication journey.

Chapter 1

So, the day the trouble starts, I'm sitting in the living room, hunched over my mystery book, when something comes ricocheting down the chimney.

Without even looking up, I can tell it's a coin—and a big one at that, judging from the dull jingle-clank it makes as it hits the concrete floor of the fireplace. I put down my book, struggle up out of the mooshy sofa, and cross the room in two long strides. Incredulous, I drop to my knees. I'm staring at John F. Kennedy, in profile. A fifty-cent piece, dated 1974.

"Wow," I say. And then, just because I'm so surprised, I say it again. "Wow."

Most fireplaces accumulate soot and ashes and charred bits of wood. Ours accumulates money. Pennies mostly, nickels and dimes sometimes, and the occasional quarter. Fifty-cent pieces? Never—until now.

The coins come at random times throughout the day, spattering down through our chimney like metal raindrops. We get non-monetary items, too. Gumballs and buttons and broken barrettes. Jellybeans at Eastertime, candy corn at Halloween. Those tiny vending machine toys that come in plastic eggs, and the plastic eggs those tiny vending machine toys come in. And peanuts. Lots of peanuts. Once I even found a meatball from Mama Rosa's Italian Kitchen.

Most people are bad aimers, which means a lot of what they throw ends up on our roof or in the yard. I de-coin the yard every day, the fireplace less often. A couple of times a year Mom gets out the ladder and uses a push broom to sweep the roof clean. We store the coins in a jumbo-sized mayonnaise jar next to the fireplace.

It's funny how some totally weird situation can start to seem normal if you live with it long enough. Like an old TV you have to smack to make the picture come on, or a teacher who calls everybody by their last name.

Or a house that's a giant wishing well.

People have been throwing coins down our chimney since I was just a little girl, and I'm twelve now. So it's become totally common and regular to me, like multivitamins or junk mail. But every now and then I take a step back and think, *Wow. This is really weird.*

And you know what? It's only the beginning of the weirdness.

Chapter 2

We live at the mall, Mom and me.

Not *near* the mall.

Not in that eight-story apartment complex *across the highway* from the mall.

Our house is literally *inside the mall.* A short way down the Farringer's wing, smack-dab in the middle of the corridor. A stone's throw from Fashion World on the right and Penny's Pretzels on the left. I will explain later how this came to be.

The mall is a two-story atrium-style structure, which means the corridors on the first level are open all the way to the skylighted ceiling. When you stand at the upper-level railing in the Farringer's wing, you can look down on our roof. Early on, somebody got the idea of trying to throw things down our chimney. The idea caught on and became a kind of tradition.

It is said that if the first coin you throw on any given day makes it into our chimney, your wish will come true.

I'm still kneeling at the fireplace when Mom comes clattering into the living room in high heels, fluffing a peach and yellow print scarf around her neck. She's getting ready to start the day at Connie's Cupboard, her little gift shop in the mall. She looks gorgeous as usual, the scarf a perfect accent to her silky yellow blouse and tan skirt.

In our household, Mom sets a fashion standard I don't even try to live up to, being a jeans and T-shirts kind of girl myself.

"Check this out," I say, holding up the coin. "JFK just came down the chimney."

She goggles in exaggerated surprise. "Wow. Somebody must have a really big wish." She peers into the oval mirror next to the front door, patting her hair discontentedly. "Darn. This stupid hair bump won't go down."

I squint at her. "What hair bump?"

"Right here." She pats harder. "It's like some weird rock formation on the side of my head. Hey, that JFK coin might be worth something. More than fifty cents, I mean." She grimaces at her reflection. "I wish I had your hair."

I go "Piff!" because I can't imagine anybody wanting my hair, least of all my mother.

Her hair is gorgeous—chestnut brown, thick, straight, orderly. Whereas mine is thousands of yellow wires bending in random directions, like dysfunctional bedsprings. I keep my hair chin-length, because if it gets even a millimeter longer, the curls begin clenching themselves into knots that only the widest-tooth comb can conquer.

"So, what's on your agenda for the day?" my mother asks, still swatting at her invisible hair bump.

I shrug. "I might run down to the bank to get some of those paper coin holders. I want to start packaging up these coins." The mayonnaise jar is nearly full. "I'll probably do some reading. Maybe start looking for school clothes."

Mom steps away from the mirror. She kisses her

fingertips, leans over the end table, and presses those kissed fingers to a framed picture of her and my dad all wet and happy at the beach. She does this every morning even though my dad's been dead for nine years.

She turns to me, frowning. "Really, Chloe? Another day indoors? You haven't seen the sun in over a week. You're going to get rickets."

"Nobody gets rickets anymore," I retort. "Not since they started putting vitamin D in milk. I looked it up on the Internet the last time you said that."

"Why don't you take the bus down to the pool, meet up with Lindy?"

"Lindy's on vacation. I told you that before."

"Well, there must be somebody you can go to the pool with," Mom persists. "Some other friend?"

I cross my arms and stare at her. There is no other friend. I keep telling her that, but it doesn't seem to be sinking in.

"You need sunshine," my mother says. "And fresh air."

"Do not make me go out in the mulch," I say ominously. "I hate it when you make me go out in the mulch."

"Just for half an hour or so."

I fling JFK into the mayonnaise jar and get to my feet. "Do you have any idea how embarrassing it is to be lying around in a lawn chair outside Deluca's Sporting Goods? People stare. They say things."

"Ignore them. You have every right to be outside in your own yard."

"But it's not my yard!" I rage. "It's Deluca's yard. If we had a normal house, I'd go outside all the time.

I'd weed flowerbeds. I'd mow the lawn. Every twelve-year-old I know mows the lawn. But me? I vacuum fake grass."

"Which reminds me," my mother says lightly. "The yard's getting salty again."

I stamp my foot. "You're not listening! I hate it here. Nobody in the whole world lives in a shopping mall except us. Why can't we move to a normal house?"

She opens her mouth and then closes it, shaking her head with a weariness I completely understand. We've had this argument so many times, we're both sick of it. She knows my part by heart—and I know hers. *There's nowhere else we could live so cheaply. We own this house free and clear, we don't have heating or cooling costs, we never have to shovel snow or mow the lawn or rake leaves...*

Mom says, "Do you want to get the lawn chair out of the cellar?"

I just stare at her. The cellar is icky. I don't go down there unless it's absolutely necessary, and sometimes not even then. She knows that.

"Fine!" she huffs. "I'll get the lawn chair. Pack up your things. Don't forget the pepper spray."

"I don't need pepper spray!" I yell. "Nobody ever tries to kidnap me. Who'd want to kidnap some crazy kid who hangs out in the mulch?"

I stomp into my bedroom and grab my backpack from the closet. The pepper spray is still inside from last time, along with a personal alarm that shrieks when you push a button. Back in the living room, I grab a banana from under the couch (more about this later) and toss it into my backpack, along with sunglasses and my mystery book. As I'm zipping my backpack shut, my mother slips in a bottle of water. Then she hands me a tube of sunscreen.

"Don't slather it on too thick. We want to make sure those vitamin D rays can get through."

By the time I've finished smearing sunscreen all over myself, Mom is on a cell phone call. I trudge outside to wait for her, slouching against the outer wall of Fashion World. I give our house a dirty look because seeing it from the outside riles me up all over again. Fifteen feet wide, fifty feet long, it's a startling sight, right here in the middle of the mall. It makes you wonder if Dorothy's house missed the exit to Oz and landed here instead.

Our house is a tiny, modest, one-story structure from the 1940s, painted yellow, its blocky shape somewhat relieved by a porch tacked on to the narrow front end. Back in the days before the house had a mall around it, there was a grassy lawn and overgrown bushes and a medium-sized maple tree out front. Now there's nothing but fake grass, the kind you might see at the bottom of a cheap plastic Easter basket.

The entire property—consisting of the house, the small back yard, and the even smaller front yard—is surrounded by a short white picket fence. The builders made the corridor extra wide to fit it all in and still leave room for shoppers to walk on either side.

My mother wanted to keep the natural greenery, but the mall bigwigs said no. They said she would not be permitted to water the lawn because the water might seep into the mall corridor and present a slipping hazard. She couldn't use a gas-powered lawn mower because the exhaust fumes would asphyxiate the shoppers. Mom, being a safety conscious individual, couldn't argue with those points. So everything in our yard got ripped out by the roots and replaced with concrete covered by synthetic grass.

"Let's go," says my mother, brushing past me with the webbed lawn chair under her arm.

As we near the intersection with the main corridor, we see a police officer striding toward the Deluca's end of the mall, where Mom's store is located. Right behind him is Ram, the daytime security guard. Ram spots us and motions for us to follow him. Ram is usually the smiliest guy in the world, but today he looks downright grim.

"Uh-oh," says Mom. "Looks like trouble."

Which pretty much sums up our lives over the next few months.

Chapter 3

"This is a despicable act of vandalism," declares Jack Caldwell, owner of the mall. "When we catch the perpetrator, we will prosecute him or her to the fullest extent of the law."

A small crowd is clustered in front of Greetings, a card shop next door to my mother's store. The policeman is there, a burly, shrewd-eyed older guy who introduces himself as Officer Sanford. He's standing next to Anna Hastings, the lady who owns Greetings. In addition, there's Ram, Jack Caldwell, a reporter from the local newspaper, a reporter and a cameraman from Channel 8 News, the proprietors of a few other nearby stores, and a handful of sweaty people wearing shorts and sneakers. And, of course, Mom and me.

Somebody egged Anna's store. The security gate, a sturdy steel grid-like structure, was in place, but the perpetrator managed to throw the eggs—seven, to be exact—through the spaces between the bars. A couple of stuffed animals, two T-shirts, and a front-facing display of cards got hit, and a porcelain vase got knocked off a shelf and smashed to smithereens.

"Who would do this?" Anna asks in a dazed, whispery voice. "It's just so mean!"

Mom gives Anna's shoulder a little squeeze. "Let's just be thankful there wasn't more damage."

"We can't say for certain when the deed was

done," Officer Sanford is telling the reporters. "We're about to start questioning the Morning Striders."

"What, you think one of them did it?" asks Ram.

"Hey!" says a sweaty gray-haired guy, taking an indignant step forward. He's wearing a T-shirt that says, "Young at heart but old in other places."

"We don't think anything at this point," the officer says, fixing his steely gaze on the sweaty guy. "You Striders get here early. We just want to know if anybody saw anything." He turns to watch a sandy-haired younger cop approach. "Find anything, Officer Pritts?"

Officer Pritts doesn't look like a policeman—his face is too gentle. I would expect him to be a veterinarian, or maybe the leader of a church youth group. In a good cop/bad cop situation, he would definitely be the good cop.

"I did a lap around the upper level," Officer Pritts says, his eyes flitting across the bystanders. "Nothing out of the ordinary up there. I checked all the entrances. There's no sign of a break-in."

Officer Sanford gives a curt nod. "Go ahead and get the evidence bagged up. If we're lucky, we'll find some fingerprints on those eggshells. I'm going to talk to these good folks about what they may or may not have seen."

Officer Pritts ducks under the yellow POLICE LINE – DO NOT CROSS tape stretched across the entrance of Greetings. Officer Sanford herds the sweaty people to a more private spot in front of a beanbag store that doesn't get much business. The reporters troop along behind them.

The Morning Striders is a fitness club whose

members are allowed to use the mall as an indoor walking track every morning between nine and ten. They have their own special entrance near the mall office, which a security guard unlocks every morning just before nine. It's the same door my mother and I use for our after-hours comings and goings, although we, unlike the Striders, have our own key.

"I don't think a Strider did this," says Anna. "Anybody could have come in that entrance." She shakes her head, and her silky red-gold hair ripples like tinted water above her shoulders. "I don't get it. Out of this whole big mall, why my store? Who has it out for me?"

"Nobody," my mother assures her. "Yours just happened to be the store that caught their eye. It could just as easily have been me."

I see her eyes wander gratefully to her own little shop. Connie's Cupboard is a fancy shoebox crammed full of goods made by artsy local people—pottery and jewelry and baskets and bookcases and baby clothes and greeting cards and floral arrangements and paintings and much, much, much, much more.

New items come in all the time, and I never stop being amazed by the creativity, the craftsmanship of the people in our area. Like, there's this amazing colorful bowl that some lady made out of magazine pages folded into tight strips and woven together. An actual bowl—made out of magazines!

The store smells like heaven, though the smells change as you mosey around. You might catch a whiff of lilac-scented bath soaps in one spot, a beachy coconut candle in the next. Or peppermint teas. Cedar planters. Potpourri made from allspice and dried rose petals.

Connie's Cupboard used to be owned by this lady named Connie Jarvis. My mother worked in the store as a salesclerk, and she and Connie became good friends. When Connie died two years ago, we were stunned to learn she had left the store to my mother.

Anna is eying the Morning Striders, three of whom are talking at the same time while Officer Sanford waves his hands, trying to shush them. "I'm going to go eavesdrop," she whispers. She sidles away.

Ram steps up, taking her place. Ram is a scrawny old guy with a head full of fluffy white hair that makes you think of Mark Twain or Albert Einstein. His full name is Random Summers, which, if you take away the capital letters, isn't a name at all—just words. Ram says his parents shared a quirky sense of humor.

"Hey, Ursula. Chloe." Ram grins his sheepish Ram-grin. "A little too much excitement for a Tuesday morning, eh?"

"For any morning," my mother says.

"Just when I thought I might make it to retirement without any major aggravation. I only got ten months left. Just want to wind down peacefully, you know what I mean?"

"I know," says my mother with a sympathetic tilt of her head.

"Hey, Urse, I been meaning to come by the shop. Anniversary's next week, and I thought maybe you could help me pick out something nice for Gloria."

My mother perks up. "I'd be happy to. She was in the store a few days ago, and I saw her admiring a certain pair of earrings. I'll put them aside for you."

"That'd be great. I'll come by later and pick them

up."

"Well. Ursula." The booming, sarcastic voice startles me. Jack Caldwell has joined us, planting himself in the space between my mother and Ram. "I would have expected the police to have you down at the station under the interrogation lights by now." He shrugs, glancing nonchalantly around the mall. "Well. I suppose it's just a matter of time before they zero in on the prime suspect."

My mother's eyes go narrow. "What are you talking about?"

Jack smiles lazily. "As they say on the cop shows, you had both opportunity and motive. Opportunity because you live right here in the mall. Motive because you and Anna are business rivals. She sells greeting cards, you sell greeting cards—am I wrong?"

"Well, of all the absurd nonsense!" blusters my mother. "Anna and I are friends, Jack. And you know perfectly well our businesses are different. She has a card shop. I sell hand-crafted items."

"Hey. Whoa." Jack holds up both hands, as if warding off a physical attack. "I'm just playing devil's advocate here. I'm not saying I think you did it. I'm just trying to see things the way the police might see them."

"Sure you are," my mother says icily.

Jack Caldwell and my mother have an uncomfortable history that dates back to high school. Long ago, when my mother was a cheerleader and Jack a football player, he asked her out. The good-looking football star always gets the pretty cheerleader, right? That's probably why my mother turned him down. She never liked doing the usual thing. Besides, she had already fallen in love with my father.

Jack Caldwell wasn't used to being rejected, and he never forgave my mother. Ever since his father retired four years ago, Jack has been running the mall, and he's always thinking up new ways to mess with us. I think that if Jack, instead of his father, had been in charge when the mall was being planned, we never would have been allowed to live here.

"See, on the surface, you and Anna would appear to be competitors," Jack goes on. "You sell the same kinds of things. Candles, floral arrangements, cards—"

"She sells commercial items," my mother snaps. "I sell hand-crafted items. They're different."

"Different, and yet the same. They're all gift items. You see what I'm saying?"

Ram is shifting uneasily from foot to foot, glancing from my mother to Jack as each one speaks.

My mother tosses her head in outrage. "This is insane. Do you really think I would egg my friend's store? You've known me since grade school, Jack. You know I don't do things like that."

"Okay, okay, point taken," says Jack. With a wicked glance at me, he adds, "So maybe your curly-haired little daughter did it. After all, she has a vested interest in whether you succeed or fail as a business owner, no?"

In an instant my mother's face goes purplish-red. She's always had this automotive-like ability to go from mildly ticked off to livid in about half a second.

"How dare you," she says in a low, snarling voice that makes me think of demon possession. "How dare you, Jack Caldwell! You can say anything you like about me. But making false accusations about my daughter? That's a low blow even for you."

Abruptly, she whirls around, turning her back on Jack. She grabs the lawn chair with one hand and my arm with the other and propels me down the corridor, past Connie's Cupboard, past Healthy You, past the dollar store. Finally she stops.

"Jack Caldwell is a big fat jerk. You know that, right?"

"I know."

She passes me the lawn chair and pecks me on the forehead. "Get out there before the sun's rays get too strong. I'll be home at lunchtime."

Chapter 4

On the east side of the mall, to the right of the Deluca's entrance, is an eight-foot by eight-foot mulchy area dotted with young shrubs, a little patch of nature wedged between the concrete sea of the parking lot and the vertical brickwork of the mall. If I close my eyes and focus on the clean, piney scent of the mulch, I can almost convince myself I'm in the middle of a forest far from civilization.

But my eyes aren't closed at the moment, so there's no forgetting where I am.

As I'm shrugging off my backpack, my hand brushes the rough exterior of the building, and I come away with three bloody knuckles. Savagely I lick the blood away, wishing my mother was here to see what a bad idea this is already turning out to be. I squish the lawn chair firmly into the mulch, being careful not to harm the shrubbery, and plop my sun-starved body into it.

I slip on my sunglasses and, with a sigh of resignation, open my book. It's nearly ten, time for the mall to open. I hear the purr of motors as cars pull into the parking spaces closest to the building. Car doors slam, and feet tramp toward the mall entrance. I smooth down my shorts and pretend to be engrossed in my book.

"Betty, look! There's a young girl in the

shrubbery."

"What on earth!"

"Must be some kind of store promotion. Maybe Deluca's has lawn chairs on sale."

"Or backpacks. Or sunglasses. You know, they really should be clearer about what they're advertising."

More feet tramp by. More voices discuss me.

"Will you look at that? Where does she think she is, the beach?"

"Kids today. They have no sense of boundaries."

"They think they own the world."

"Let's find mall security. We're reporting this."

Go ahead, report me, I want to yell. Ram couldn't care less that I'm in the mulch. In fact, he encourages it. He's always saying kids need to spend time outdoors every day getting sunshine and fresh air.

Although my book is intriguing, I can't concentrate on it. I keep thinking about what Jack Caldwell said, that my mom is a prime suspect. I can see how it might look that way to someone who doesn't know her. I just hope the police catch the real vandal soon so Mom doesn't have to go through the humiliation of being investigated.

After fifteen minutes, I get thirsty, so I take a long swig of water. I consider eating my banana but decide I'd rather not do it in public, like a monkey in the zoo. I'll save it for later. Not too much later, though. Right now it's the perfect shade of pale yellow-green, but it won't stay that way for long.

Mom and I prefer our bananas at a particular stage of unripeness, when you get the feeling they're still holding back. If we wait till they turn deep yellow, the flavor is too intense for our liking. Too rich, too sweet.

We Lamont women like our ’nanas bland.

I adjust the lawn chair to the completely reclined position and flip over to give my backside its fair share of grilling. Chloe Lamont, human hamburger. I close my eyes and breathe in that mulchy scent, only now it’s tinged with the toxic odor of car exhaust fumes.

My watch alarm goes off at ten twenty-seven. With relief I gather up my belongings and head back inside—hot, sweaty, and all dosed up with vitamin D.

As I approach my house, I glance upward. Two boys around my age are leaning over the balcony railing, throwing peanuts-in-the-shell at our chimney.

“Hey!” I yell. “Stop that!”

They either don’t hear me or choose to ignore me.

I drop the lawn chair and my backpack on the front porch and walk around the yard, picking up coins, a chore I never got around to doing last night because I got engrossed in a TV movie. The synthetic grass rustles like crepe paper beneath my sandals. My mother is right—the yard is salty again. I make a mental note to vacuum it later, after the mall closes.

Our yard tends to suffer regular, dandruff-like accumulations of salt from Penny’s Pretzels, just across the way. How that salt gets from Penny’s to our yard is a mystery. I mean, it’s not like it wafts over on ocean breezes.

And it’s not just salt that comes over. So does the yeasty smell of pretzels, the spicy scent of pepperoni. Those smells gather in our yard like smoke and seep through cracks and crevices into our house. I swear they’re stuck to the very walls, as permanent as paint.

Most people would say the scent of a freshly baked pretzel is a good smell. But try smelling it every single day for seven years. Honestly, I never want to eat a soft pretzel again.

I work quickly, shoving coins into the pockets of my shorts. A peanut rolls off the roof and pings me on the head. I can feel people staring but I don't make eye contact. I don't like to hang out in my yard during mall hours because it makes me feel like an exotic animal being observed in its natural habitat. But I have to pick up these coins, because if I don't do it, other people will. Kids, especially. We constantly catch them reaching through our fence to snatch up whatever coinage they can reach.

The mall is busy today. But then, when isn't it? My eyes hug the ground as I hunt for coins, but I can't block out the blur of color at the edges of my vision. It's everywhere—in the clothes of the passing shoppers, the vivid displays of merchandise. The lit-up store signs. Sometimes I wish I could tone down all that color, flick a switch and turn the mall world to grayscale.

Then there's the never-ending noise. The buzz of conversation, punctuated now and then by the furious wail of a toddler or the excited shriek of a teenager. The competing music—rap songs pulsing from Denim Den, two stores down to our left, and pop tunes drifting out of Fashion World, to our immediate right.

Mom says what I'm experiencing is sensory overload, and sometimes she feels it, too. It's always a relief when nighttime comes and everything goes dim and quiet.

It takes me ten minutes to de-coin the yard. I end up with eighty-some cents, mostly in pennies but with some nickels, too. After emptying my pockets into the mayonnaise jar, I take a shower and go to my room.

I scowl at the mural on the wall opposite my bed, a white picket fence with sunflowers drooping over it and, in the distance, a green hill with a big, leafy tree at the top. My mother painted that mural when I was five. I know she was trying to give me a sense of the outdoors that was missing in my life. But while I appreciate her efforts, two-dimensional artwork isn't doing it for me anymore.

At seven past twelve my mother comes through the front door, a flurry of swirling skirt and flying hair.

"Just in time for lunch," I say.

"You made lunch?" Her smile is radiant.

Just as we step into the kitchen, the doorbell rings. We exchange apprehensive looks. Are the police after us already?

Chapter 5

It's only Ram at the door.

"Ursula, I'm sorry to bother you at lunchtime, honey," he says, stepping inside. "I just wanted to tell you about the latest development."

"Development?"

"The police are saying the egg attack happened in the middle of the night. They can tell because of how congealed the egg yolks are. They brought in an expert."

My mother raises an eyebrow. "The police have a congealed egg expert?"

"Something like that. Anyhow, they're saying the eggs were probably thrown between midnight and two a.m."

My mother is frowning and blinking, blinking and frowning as she processes this new information.

Ram puts a hand on her arm, looking earnest. "Ursula, you know I'm not trying to be devil's avatar or whatever, like Jack Caldwell, right? I just want you to have all the facts."

Mom nods dully. "Nobody's in the mall between midnight and two a.m. except Chloe and me and whatever security guard is on duty."

"I know." Ram bows his head, acknowledging this disturbing fact. "But plenty of people have keys. Jack, the general manager, the office supervisor. All the non-duty guards. Plus, there's a spare key in the office that anybody could have taken."

He looks from Mom to me. "Did you two go out last night? Because we're thinking maybe the last person who went in or out forgot to lock the door."

My mother shakes her head. "Chloe and I haven't left the mall in over a week."

She stares pensively at Ram for a moment and then asks, "What about the security cameras? Didn't anything show up on them?"

Ram drops his gaze. "Actually, the cameras are out of commission just now. Whole system went down a couple weeks back. We told Jack, but he's been so busy building that new mall over in Clifton, he hasn't gotten around to doing anything about it."

My mother makes a huffy noise. "That is so typical! Jack doesn't care about this mall. He never has. Not like his father did."

"Aw, now, Urse," Ram murmurs, patting her arm. "Thing is, even if the cameras were working, they might not have picked up anything. We only got a few of 'em, mostly at the main entrances and corridor intersections. It's not like they cover every square inch of the mall."

"Well, why not?" demands my mother. "Why isn't Jack doing a better job of monitoring what goes on around here? He has a responsibility to keep everybody safe."

"Yeah…" Ram fidgets a little. "You know, you really can't blame Jack for that. Parker and his partners, they were the ones that decided about security cameras and whatnot, back when the mall was being built. They didn't think we needed a lot, considering the low crime rate in this area. Anyhow, I'm betting you this was just a one-time thing, something some kids did on a lark."

"I hope you're right, Ram."

"Me too, Urse. Me too." Ram moves toward the door. "Don't you worry. The police will figure things out. I'll see you two later."

****

"This looks delicious," Mom says, gazing across our nicked-up wooden table, which is crowded with the elements of our lunch—two deli-turkey sandwiches on plates, two bowls of chicken noodle soup, a bowl filled with potato chips for us to share, and two glasses of iced tea.

I don't usually make lunch for Mom, because she almost always packs her lunch and eats at the store, standing behind the counter and taking discreet nibbles between customers. But when she said she'd be home at lunchtime, I thought I should do something nice for her. Because today of all days she surely needs it.

"I was going to make omelets," I tell her. "But there was only one egg."

Her spoon clatters to the table. "One egg? That's impossible. I bought a whole dozen just a few days ago."

"Well, there's only one there now."

"Okay. Let's see." She starts counting on her fingers. "I used three eggs to make that quiche on Sunday."

"You made banana bread yesterday. That's one more, right?"

She stares into the air. "Four eggs. That's all I've used." She looks hopefully at me. "Did you use any?"

I shake my head.

"So minus the one that's left, that leaves seven unaccounted for," she says.

I gasp. "That's how many got smashed in Anna's store!"

We stare at each other in mutual dismay.

"It's just a weird coincidence," she says in a shaky, high-pitched voice. "This has nothing to do with what happened at Greetings."

"But where did our eggs go? Eggs don't just disappear."

"Not usually," she says faintly.

"Do you think we should tell the police about this?"

She thinks that over and then shakes her head. "I don't think it would help. It would just make us look guilty. And we're not guilty, right?"

It bothers me that she put a question mark at the end of that.

Chapter 6

It must be a slow news day, because when the Channel 8 people walk past our house, they're reminded of the long-ago controversy and decide to do a nine-years-later kind of story.

My mother and I meet a reporter and a cameraman outside our house at two o'clock. Passing shoppers eye us curiously, and some stop to watch. We face the camera, our house in the background, while the reporter, Lisa Manning, speaks into her microphone.

"I'm standing in front of the home of Ursula and Chloe Lamont. An ordinary-looking house, to be sure—except that it happens to be inside the Oasis Mall. It's been nine years since construction began on the mall. As you may recall…"

And then she sums up the events that led to this bizarre arrangement.

Nine years ago my parents and I were living in this very house in a normal neighborhood with my dad's dad, Glen Lamont. For more than a year Glen had been in a legal battle with real estate developer Parker Caldwell—Jack Caldwell's father—and his partners, who had picked our neighborhood as the perfect spot to build a shopping mall. They bought up all the houses and vacant land except for the small lot and modest home owned by Glen.

Glen had been born and raised in that house, and he

and his late wife, Marge, raised their son—my father, Greg—there. Glen refused to sell. He said he wasn't about to leave the home he'd lived in all his life.

Both sides were very stubborn, but it looked like Glen was going to lose. Parker got the city officials on his side, and they said that Parker could buy Glen's property whether Glen wanted to sell or not. A law called eminent domain allows this if there is a good reason, and in this case the reason was economic development.

What that meant was, the mall was expected to attract lots of shoppers and their money, which would be good for our town. So my parents and Grandpa Glen were told they would have to move.

Then my father died. He was a city firefighter. A burning apartment building collapsed while he was inside. The collapse happened right after he'd handed a small child out the window. He was the only person who died in the fire, and if it hadn't been for him, that small child would have died instead.

Around this same time, my grandfather was diagnosed with terminal lung cancer. So there we were, a brand-new widow, a three-year-old child, and a dying man, about to be kicked out of our home just so some rich real estate developers could build their fancy new mall.

Sometimes I look back through the newspapers my mother saved from that time. One has a picture of me, my mom, and my grandpa on the front page. My mother, her face pinched with grief and worry, is holding me on one hip while a haggard Glen leans against her opposite shoulder, as if he can't support his own weight. I'm staring into the camera, my blonde curls tousled, my mouth open in a grimace of anguish.

The mayor of the city, John Tomlinson, saw how things would look if we got kicked out of our home. He was up for re-election in a few months and was afraid people wouldn't vote for him if he allowed the family of a dead firefighter—one who'd died a hero—to be forced out of their home.

It was Mayor Tomlinson who proposed that Parker build his mall around our house. Everybody thought he was joking at first. But he wasn't. Mayor Tomlinson was a creative thinker, somebody known for his quirky solutions to problems.

What followed were countless meetings involving attorneys and city council members and zoning officials and architects. In the end, Mayor Tomlinson's idea was approved. The contract said we could live in the mall until I graduated from high school or until we chose to leave, whichever came first.

Meanwhile, Parker and his partners came to realize that all the publicity was going to be very good for business. The mall would be a tourist attraction. People would come from all around to see the fully intact house nestled in the middle of the mall—and maybe catch a glimpse of the tragic little family who lived there. And while they were at the mall, they were bound to spend money.

My memory of that time is hazy. The workers put a giant sheet over our house to keep out the dirt and dust. I remember trying to look out the windows and seeing only white, as if we were lost in a swirling snowstorm. And I remember the noise. Pounding, jack-hammering, drilling, the shouted conversations of workers. I was five when the mall was finally completed. Grandpa

Glen died six weeks before the Grand Opening.

For the first couple of months, my mother and I were celebrities. People lined up along our fence, snapping pictures as we came outside. We were known as the Oasis Mall Family. Some of the stores gave us gifts—bedspreads, drinking glasses, certificates for free haircuts. Zeke's Electronics gave me a radio-controlled car. Farringer's department store outfitted me in a red wool winter coat with a matching hat.

Slowly we adjusted to our new surroundings. Our old neighbors had been the Wilsons, the Croccos, and the Merrimans. Our new ones were Fashion World, Discount Cell Phones, and Penny's Pretzels.

Lisa Manning finishes rehashing the story of the Oasis Mall Family and turns to my mother. "I understand you own a store here in the mall."

My mother tells how she inherited the store from Connie and what a good person and a wonderful friend Connie was.

I have to fight back a wave of sadness because I still miss Connie. She was the closest thing I had to a grandma. Well—sort of. My mother's parents are living, but I've never met them. They live far away, though I don't know where. Mom had a big fight with them years ago, and she won't talk about them except to say they're evil.

Connie's only child never had children of his own, so technically Connie wasn't a grandma. Yet she was mine through and through. She always listened when I talked, and she would give me little presents for no reason—dainty silver necklaces, Christmas socks with goofy, cross-eyed reindeer on them, my very own Young Miss Nail Care Kit. Her hugs made me feel like

I was swaddled in flannel and sitting in front of a crackling fire.

Although Connie's Cupboard had been part of the mall since opening day, we didn't really get to know Connie until I was eight. For the first three years after my dad died, my mother didn't have a job. She felt it was important to be home with me, so we lived off the life insurance money.

When I started first grade, Mom got a part-time job as a secretary at an insurance agency in a neighboring borough—and just in time, too, because the insurance money was almost gone by then. She worked from nine o'clock to two-thirty every day, which meant she could put me on the school bus in the morning and be home in time to meet it every afternoon.

That worked out great for two years. Then the car died. The problem was major, something to do with the transmission. We didn't have the money to fix it. With no way to get to work, Mom lost her job.

I remember that day—the day she lost her job. We were in the kitchen, and she was making chocolate chip cookies, trying to act like everything was fine. She was digging hardened brown sugar out of the bag when her plastic measuring spoon snapped.

Suddenly she was crying. Hard. She said I'd better get used to never having home-baked goods in the house because the most important measuring spoon of all, the tablespoon, had just broken, and we couldn't afford to buy a new set of spoons.

I led her to the couch and tucked blankets around her. I made her tea. I told her I would be back in a few minutes, and I left the house. I went to the dollar store, where I bought a new set of measuring spoons with my own money.

When I came home, I handed her the dollar store bag. When she saw the measuring spoons inside, she started crying harder than ever, but in a different way. It was a kind of hysterical happiness. She hugged me and said everything was going to be okay.

Later she told me that at that moment she no longer felt as if she had the weight of the whole world on her shoulders. She realized that at eight I was already a strong, resourceful human being, someone she could count on.

I mentioned that I'd seen a "Help Wanted, Salesclerk" sign in the window of Connie's Cupboard. Later that day, Mom went down and applied for the job. She started work the next day, and Connie pretty much took us under her wing. And that was when our lives started to turn around.

Lisa Manning shoves her microphone in my face. "And how do you like living at the mall?"

I can feel my mother tense up next to me.

"It's great," I say, maybe a little too enthusiastically. "What kid wouldn't love living at the mall?"

"If it wasn't for school, you'd never have to leave," Lisa Manning says with a smile. "Everything you need is right here."

She's right about that. The summer the car died we didn't leave the mall for two months. We didn't have to—all the important places are here. Our bank, two hair salons, the Shop and Save supermarket, four major department stores. Restaurants and movie theaters and a drug store. Even Mom's eye doctor is here. In a way, the mall is like an indoor town, a self-contained ecosystem.

Lisa Manning thanks us for talking with her and tells us to be sure to watch our interview on the six o'clock news.

At five-thirty Mom brings home takeout from Mama Rosa's. She forgot dessert, but fruit will do, so I go hunting for bananas. I find one in the bathroom, on the toilet tank, plus there's still the one in my backpack.

You will always find bananas in strange places at our house. It's because my mother once read an article that said bananas last longer if you separate them. Bananas give off a gas that helps them ripen. If six bananas are bunched together, that's a whole lot of banana-ripening gas floating around. One banana by itself produces less gas, so it doesn't go bad as fast. That's the theory, anyway.

Every bunch of bananas we buy immediately gets torn apart, like a litter of puppies being split up. We stash bananas in random locations throughout the house—on the fireplace mantel, on a windowsill, under the couch, in my sock drawer. Sometimes we lose track of them until we smell that sweetish rotting scent or see the telltale swarm of fruit flies.

We watch ourselves on the six o'clock news as we eat our bananas. What was a ten-minute interview has been whittled down to less than a minute, but in my opinion we both come across as intelligent and likable.

"Come on," my mother says when our segment is over. "Let's go shopping for school clothes."

I'm not about to say no to that. I dash to my room to grab my purse.

"Living at the mall?" I say as we head out the door. "Sometimes it's not so bad."

Chapter 7

I'm in the cave again, in the middle of a passageway. I don't know which way to go because I don't know where I came from. My flashlight makes shadows on the bumpy walls, eerie patterns of movement I keep catching from the corner of my eye.

I know there are spiders down here, big as a grown man's hand. They are furtive, bloodthirsty creatures that hate the light. As long as I have my flashlight, they will stay away. But my light is dim, and if the batteries die...

I need to get out of here. Now. I take a step forward. There's a noise behind me, a brittle scrambling sound, maybe just a bit of the rocky wall crumbling away. But because I'm already on edge, I whirl around, and as I do, I lose my grip on the flashlight. It clunks to the rocky floor, the light flicking off abruptly. I am left in complete darkness.

Almost at once it begins, the breathy scurrying of thousands of feet. The spiders swarm over me, tickling my skin with their hairy legs, clinging to my arms, crawling under my shirt, burrowing into my hair, and I'm screaming, screaming...

I scream myself awake. I'm in my own room, which is daytime-bright from the skylighted mall corridor outside my window. I lie still for a few minutes, waiting for my heart to settle down.

The spider nightmare. Ugh. I used to have it all the time when I was little, around the time the mall was being built. These days it comes only when I'm anxious about something. Like starting school or being a possible suspect in a crime investigation.

I sit up slowly, like a recovering invalid, and give my stomach a good hard scratch to relieve the spider-itchiness that followed me out of the dream. I glance at the clock on my nightstand. It's ten-twenty. It was nice of Mom to let me sleep in, but I kind of wish she hadn't. If I'd gotten up earlier, I could have avoided the nightmare.

I eat a leisurely breakfast at the kitchen table—a piece of peanut butter toast and a bowl of corn flakes topped with sliced bananas. As I eat, I flip through a ladies' magazine my mother left on the table. The cheerful photos and upbeat articles chase away the last bits of nightmare creepiness.

Talk drifts through the open window. Snips of conversation from the speed walkers—

"…just not sure I want to get married."

"Well, you'd better get sure pretty quick. The wedding's next week!"

Intriguing little half-stories I want to hear more of—

"…so there I am, buck naked in a bus shelter at three a.m., waiting for Sam to come get me, when, wouldn't you know it, a police car pulls up…"

And the near side of cell phone conversations—

"Mom, I told you. I'm at school…Yes, I am! I'm standing outside Remedial Calculus at this very moment. Why won't you believe me?"

The talk that blows by is mildly entertaining, but

what I'd really like to hear is outdoor noise. Bird twitter, the rustling of treetops, the rumble and swish of passing cars. I'd love to see the curtains inhaling and exhaling the breeze, not just hanging limply in the stagnant mall air.

I'm halfway to the sink with my dirty dishes when the doorbell rings. I give a start. Milk sloshes out of my cereal bowl and hits the floor with a soft splat.

Is this how it's going to be every time somebody comes to the door? Wondering if that shrewd-eyed cop is on the other side?

I open the door a crack and then fling it wide. "Uncle Ron!"

"Hey, kiddo." He steps through the doorway and enfolds me in his arms.

Technically, Ron Caldwell isn't my uncle any more than Connie was my grandma. He's just an old family friend. Brown-haired, brown-eyed, moderate and average and ordinary in every way. But oh so nice.

Ron is Jack Caldwell's cousin but is nothing like Jack. After my dad died, Ron took care of us for a while. He helped my mom sort out her finances, took my grandpa for his cancer treatments, and babysat me when Mom had appointments with her attorney or the life insurance company or the social security people. Our lives have settled down since then, but Ron still pops in fairly often to see how we're doing.

Like Jack, Ron is a real estate developer. This line of work runs in their family. It's what their fathers, who are brothers, did. It's what their grandfather did.

Jack runs the mall as well as a nearby industrial park, and he's building a mall in Clifton, a neighboring town. Ron owns many of the buildings in downtown

Willowdale—stores and restaurants and apartment buildings. Ron and Jack are the same age, and they both went to school with my mother.

"Look at you," says Ron, stepping back to take in the whole length of me. "Growing like a weed. Before long you'll be passing me up."

Which isn't saying much. Both Ron and his cousin Jack ended up at the short end of the height chart. Whereas I seem to be turning out medium-sized like my parents.

We get situated in the living room, Ron on the couch, me in the rocking chair.

Ron says, "I heard there was some trouble yesterday. Vandalism, huh?"

"Yeah. Greetings got egged."

I'm debating whether to tell him about our missing eggs but decide not to when he starts talking again. "You know, I'm always trying to talk your mom into moving downtown. I have a beautiful storefront that just went vacant. It would be perfect for Connie's Cupboard. The best part is, there are condos for sale in the same building. Windows on all sides, a big balcony out back. You could live right above the store. It would be better than being stuck in this stuffy old mall."

"It sounds great." I let myself dream for a moment, picturing a lawn chair stretched out on my own private balcony. Rain-scented breezes wafting through open windows. A coin-free fireplace. "But I don't think we can afford a condo."

"Sure you can. Your mother's doing very well for herself. And I'd be willing to give her a break on the price. A very good break." He shrugs. "But, hey. Maybe you like living here."

"I do not like living here," I say vehemently. "Mom, though—she's a different story."

Ron winks. "Maybe between the two of us we can bring her around. I'm heading down to Connie's now to take her to lunch. Just wanted to stop in to say hi to my favorite niece."

****

"Do you even know what a condo is?" asks my mother, frowning down at her paring knife. She's speed-slicing cucumbers, her forceful movements conveying her irritation. "You're always saying you want to move to a different house. But a condo isn't a house. It's more like an apartment."

"But we would own it like a house," I point out. "And it has a big balcony and lots of windows. The best part is, it wouldn't be in this stuffy old mall."

She grabs a handful of cucumber slices and throws them in the salad bowl. She's bustling around like there's an emergency, which there isn't. She's home for the evening. Vanessa, her part-time salesclerk, is in charge of the store. "We can't afford to buy our own place right now. I've told you that before."

"Ron says you can afford it."

She looks at me in exasperation. "And how would he know?"

"He says he'd give you a really good deal on the condo. He says—"

"Ron says, Ron says." She shakes her head. "I can't believe he's doing this. Trying to use you to get to me."

"He isn't! Ron's our friend. He's trying to help us."

She's chopping a tomato now, though it looks more like murder. Pulp and seeds are flying everywhere. "I don't want to hear any more about this."

"But did he tell you about that empty store? He says—"

"Chloe! That's enough."

A few moments later, in a voice that sounds almost normal, she says, "Could you run down to Shop and Save after dinner? We need bananas. Oh, and we're out of eggs."

"I know," I say crossly. "I know we're out of eggs."

Chapter 8

Today's the day. Lindy's coming home.

It's the first thing I think of when I wake up. In fact, I don't think I ever stopped thinking about it all night long. I can hardly wait to find out if we're going to be in the same seventh-grade section.

In our junior high, they group kids by scholastic ability so everybody can learn at the pace that works best for them. It's kind of like the Sorting Hat in *Harry Potter.* There are eight seventh-grade sections, seven-one through seven-eight. They put the brightest kids in seven-one, the next-to-the-brightest in seven-two, and so on.

Mom thinks this is a terrible practice. She says it's like the school is telling the kids in the bottom groups that not much is expected of them.

I think I agree with her. Being assigned to seven-seven or seven-eight would be like getting sorted into Hufflepuff.

Not that I was worried I'd end up in one of the bottom groups. My grades have always been really good, except for in kindergarten, when I kept getting Needs Improvement in areas like "Makes relevant contributions to class discussions" and "Willing to take risks and try new things."

Anyway, my schedule came in the mail a few days ago. I made it into seven-one!

When I told Mom, she let out a shriek and hugged me. I said, "I thought you hated the way the school groups kids by how smart they are." She said, "I do. I'd hate it more if you were in seven-eight."

We went out to dinner to celebrate—not to one of the mall places, but to a real restaurant, a fancy steak and seafood place five miles away.

I'm jittery all morning, hoping and praying Lindy made it into seven-one. Because if she didn't, I'll never see her. And that would be a disaster, considering she's my only real friend.

Here's what I've tried to explain to my mother. You can't expect someone who's spent her formative years in a shopping mall to have a ton of friends. Neighborhoods—not malls—are where friendships are born. You have to be within walking distance of people.

I know about neighborhoods because I've been to Lindy's. It's overrun with kids whose personal histories are woven together, making them more like sisters and brothers than neighbors. They're nice to me when I visit, but I can't help feeling left out when they start reminiscing—"Hey, remember when we soaped Old Man Branson's windows and he chased us down the street with that pointy umbrella?" Even their tales of second-degree sunburns and mass groundings make me envious.

I'm not saying a neighborhood is the only place friendships can bloom. But that's where they grow best.

My friendship with Lindy started at school. Her family moved to our town last summer, and we showed up on the first day of sixth grade wearing identical shoes, white sneakers with lavender stripes. We started talking—okay, technically *she* started talking to *me*—

and discovered we liked a lot of the same things. The singer Taylor Swift, mystery books, and Persian cats. Also ballroom dancing—watching, not doing. And old-fashioned board games, the kind you might find in a beat-up box in somebody's grandma's attic.

The thing about Lindy, though, the thing that has always bothered me, is that she attracts friends the way overripe bananas attract fruit flies. She might be my only friend, but I'm not hers. If I'm not physically close to her all day at school like I was last year, she'll simply make friends with the people who are. I will be bumped out of her life.

Lindy calls at eleven a.m.

"Yay, you're baaaack!" I say, practically singing the words.

"I'm baaaack!" she says, mimicking my tone. "We actually got home yesterday. Our neighborhood was having this block party, and Mom and Dad made us go. We were there till almost midnight. I just woke up."

You got home yesterday? Why didn't you call me? That's what I think, but what I say is, "So did you get your schedule? What section are you in?"

"Oh, right—the schedule. I'm in seven-two."

Dismay hits me like a fist in the stomach. "Seven-two? Oh, no! I'm in seven-one."

"Whoa. Check you out. One of the smarties." Her tone is light and teasing, and I'm hurt that she doesn't sound upset.

"Marina's in seven-two." Lindy is chattering on. "So are Brynne and Darcy. Oh, and Jason B. Marina was telling me at the cookout last night."

"Do you know anybody in seven-one?" I ask bleakly.

"Ashley Elizabeth, I think. And some of those really brainy kids, the ones who always get picked for Scholastic Quiz. Probably some kids from West End, too."

There are two elementary schools in our district—East End, which Lindy and I attended, and West End—but only one junior high school and one high school. Kids from East End and West End get thrown together for the first time in seventh grade. So our class is about to double in size, and half of our classmates will be strangers to us.

Eventually Lindy and I discover that we have lunch at the same time. That's something, I guess. We make plans to eat together.

"So, tell me about your vacation," I say, trying to push past my despair.

Lindy's parents are teachers, so they always have the whole summer off. This year they decided to spend a month touring national landmarks and teaching their four kids about the history of our great nation.

"Well," says Lindy, "I learned there are four presidents on Mount Rushmore." She giggles. "But don't ask me who they are, because I don't remember."

Lindy hates how her parents try to turn every experience into an educational one. She rebels by letting as little knowledge as possible accumulate in her brain.

"I don't know either," I say, though I do. George Washington, Thomas Jefferson, Theodore Roosevelt, and Abraham Lincoln.

But I don't want to sound like a seven-one smarty.

Chapter 9

When the doorbell rings, Mom is in the kitchen, doing the supper dishes. Our kitchen is too tiny to accommodate a dishwasher, so we take turns washing dishes in the sink.

"I'll get it," I call from the living room, putting down my book and wondering yet again if the police have come to question us.

But it's not the police. Standing on my porch is Lonnie Davis from school and a tall, red-haired girl I've never seen before. I am startled to the point of speechlessness. Lonnie is one of the popular girls, and she's never bothered with me. In fact, she has a way of looking straight through me that makes me wonder if I've gone invisible.

"Hi, Chloe," Lonnie says, glancing around to see if any passersby are watching.

"Hi," I say warily.

"My cousin from New Jersey is visiting, and I thought I'd bring her to the mall."

I glance from Lonnie to her cousin, waiting for a formal introduction, but Lonnie doesn't seem to think that's necessary.

"So, how was your summer?" Lonnie asks in a chit-chatty tone.

The cousin is leaning to the right, a faint smile of intrigue on her face as she tries to peer into my house. I step to the side, blocking her view.

"Good," I say.

"Are you excited about seventh grade? I am. What section are you in?"

"Seven-one."

"I'm in seven-three. Hey, you want to come shopping with us?"

"I'm kind of busy," I say.

"Oh. Okay. I guess I'll see you at school then."

As I'm shutting the door, my mother comes into the living room, drying her hands on a tea towel. "Who was that at the door?"

"Some girl from school. And her cousin."

"Why didn't you go shopping with them? I heard them ask you."

I consider making up an excuse and then decide to go with the truth. "Because—because they're not interested in me! Lonnie was just showing off to her cousin that she knows some weird girl who lives at the mall. It happens all the time."

"If all she wanted to do was show off," Mom says, "she wouldn't have asked you to go shopping."

I roll my eyes. "She knew I'd say no. She never even talks to me at school."

Mom flings the tea towel onto the back of the couch. "Those girls reached out to you, Chloe. You should have reached back. That's how you make friends."

"I don't need to make friends. I already have friends." Well, one friend, anyway.

"You push people away," she says. "I've seen it time and time again."

"I do not push people away."

"No? Take a look through your school yearbooks. In every single picture, you're scowling."

"I am not!"

"Your expression says, 'Keep away from me.' It says, 'Don't even try to talk to me, because I'll bite your head off.' "

Okay, so maybe I push people away. But only some people. Only the jerks—like Lonnie, like Jason Bingham. In third grade, Jason started picking on me, calling me Mall Goon. He made fun of me every single day. He got other kids doing it, too. Mostly boys, but also some of the meaner girls.

Every day at recess, a group of them would circle me on the playground while they called out taunts.

"Hey, Mall Goon—what's on sale this week?"

"You can always tell when Mall Goon's mother is frying onions. The whole mall stinks."

"Did you know when it's real quiet, you can hear Mall Goon flush her toilet?"

I was mortified. I told my mother I hated onions so she would stop frying them. I made sure our bathroom window was always closed, and even so, I cringed every time I flushed.

And then one day a couple of snickering boys clomped up onto my porch, Jason among them. I was in the living room, but maybe they thought nobody was home, because they cupped their hands around their eyes and tried to peer in the window. And that's when I burst out the front door. Our broom happened to be propped against the banister. I grabbed it and started swinging at the boys like a deranged orangutan.

"Get off my porch, you stupid jerks! You're on private property. We just called mall security, and you're all getting arrested!"

That did the trick. The boys stumbled backward, and one of them fell off the porch. They probably figured that if I was home, my mom was, too, and they did not want to tangle with an angry grown-up. They sprinted down the sidewalk and through the gate, disappearing into the crowd of shoppers.

The teasing eased up after that, but I had a feeling it was because word had gotten around that I was crazy. Maybe dangerously so.

"It's true. You push people away," Mom says.

I don't like the way this conversation is going, so I decide to turn the tables. "Yeah? Well, if I do, it's because I learned it from you. You don't exactly have friends breaking down the door."

My mother looks taken aback. "I have friends. Anna and I are close, and Ram—"

"They're not friends. They're people you see at work. It's not like you go to the movies with them or have them over for dinner."

Mom tosses her head in that impatient, you-don't-understand way I've seen so many times before. "You know how busy I am with the store. I don't have time for socializing."

"Other people have stores, but they socialize. Connie used to say—" I break off.

"What?" demands my mother. "What did Connie say?"

Connie said a lot of things. Once when I was complaining because my mother wouldn't take me to the mall Christmas party, Connie sat me down and explained some things. She said my mother had been hurt so many times, she went through life like an abused dog, expecting more of the same. Connie called her a battered soul.

My mother didn't trust people, and that was why she kept mostly to herself. She had grown a hard shell around her—not a turtle shell she could pop in and out of, but an armadillo shell that served as a shield while she snapped at attackers with her sharp teeth.

But I can't tell my mother these things, because they were between Connie and me.

"Connie said…you push people away," I finally say.

My mother is silent for a few moments. Then she says, "Maybe I do. Maybe we both do. And maybe it's time we stopped."

"Maybe it is," I say.

She nods toward the door. "If you hurry, you can probably catch up with them."

I shake my head. "No. Lonnie Davis is not somebody I'm going to go chasing after. But next time somebody comes to the door—we'll see."

Chapter 10

"Good morning!" says Miss Chappell. "Welcome to Accelerated English!"

Miss Chappell is a new teacher at Crawford Heights Junior High, and new is exactly how she looks. As in just graduated from college. She's a young, slim Black lady, with long hair barretted into a low ponytail. Today, the first day of school, she's wearing a denim skirt and a pale-yellow T-shirt that is just the sort of thing I would wear myself.

In fact, our outfits are sort of alike. I'm wearing brand-new jeans that project just the right degree of chewed-by-wild-dogs, and a pale-orange T-shirt that accentuates the modest tan I built during those summer mornings in the mulch.

All of Miss Chappell's talk comes out in this fast up-and-down voice, like she just won the lottery and her prize is that she gets to teach seventh-grade English.

"We'll be doing a lot of reading this year," she says. "And writing. I'd like to form our reading groups today. Let's see... We have twenty-two students, so that works out to two groups of five and two groups of six."

People start craning around in their seats, making eye contact with friends and mouthing *You wanna be in my group?*

The only person who makes eye contact with me is

a new kid named Robby Morales. He's been staring at me all morning. I let my eyes skim past him like I don't notice.

I look around at all the smart people and wonder what I'm doing in seven-one. There's no one I can picture myself being friends with. Half the people are West Enders, so I don't even know them. The other half are East Enders, so I do know them. And that's a whole different problem.

"Before we can form groups," Miss Chappell continues, "we have to pick our genres. Can anyone tell me what genre means?"

Ashley Elizabeth Hutzell's hand shoots up. "It means what kind of book it is. Like romance. That's a genre."

"Exactly!" says Miss Chappell. "Genre simply means category. And romance is a great example. Romance books can have other elements—adventure, intrigue, comedy—but they are first and foremost love stories."

Ashley Elizabeth tosses her head in her usual haughty way.

Ashley Elizabeth insists on being called Ashley Elizabeth. That's six syllables' worth of name, and saying it makes you feel like you're chewing overbaked fruitcake. At the start of each school year, some unsuspecting teacher inevitably calls her Ashley and wonders why she doesn't respond. Until someone pipes up helpfully, "You have to call her Ashley Elizabeth."

Last year she sat behind me in math class, and I called her Ash. She corrected me maybe eighty-seven times before she realized I wasn't going to back down. I think I'm the only person who gets away with this.

Ash isn't a natural beauty, but the overall package is very good-looking. Her parents have money, and they put a lot of it into their daughter's appearance. Ash wears designer clothes, and her shoes always look brand-new. She has thick, bouncy, honey-brown hair that looks like it was transplanted from a movie star's head. It's the same hair her mother has, and you can tell the two of them take great pride in it.

"So what we want to do," Miss Chappell is saying, "is choose four genres and then form our groups around them. You won't necessarily be in a group with your closest friends. The goal is to get each of you in a group with others who enjoy the same sort of reading material that you do."

She sends a brave smile around the classroom. Then she steps backward to the dry erase board and picks up a blue marker. "Let's brainstorm for genres. Just start calling them out."

"Romance!" says Ash, and Miss Chappell writes Romance on the board.

"Vampire stories!" cries Tara Leibowitz.

"Too specific," says Miss Chappell. "Let's call that one Horror." She writes Horror on the board.

"Zombies!" says Gabe Felton.

"Also Horror," says Miss Chappell.

"Mystery!" I call out.

"Good one!" says Miss Chappell. She scrawls Mystery on the board.

The ideas keep coming. Some of them technically aren't genres, but Miss Chappell writes them down anyway.

"Science Fiction!"

"Thriller!"

"Paranormal!"

"Comic books!"

"Harry Potter!"

"Fantasy!"

"Serial killers!"

"Comedy!"

Before long, the board is covered in genres. They're scrawled at random angles, the way people sign a school yearbook.

Miss Chappell helps us weed out the non-genres, leaving us with ten solid categories. Then we vote for our favorites. The four genres we end up with are Romance, Horror, Mystery, and Science Fiction. I'm pleased that my category is one of the winners.

Miss Chappell assigns a corner of the classroom to each of the genres. We're supposed to go to the area that most interests us.

There are twelve girls and ten boys in the class. Seven of the girls immediately shoot over to Romance, while four girls and three boys plant themselves firmly in Horror—and you can tell by who the girls are that they're thinking vampires in love. I'm in Mystery, along with the new kid, Robby Morales. Six boys make up the Sci Fi group.

"That's a good start," says Miss Chappell. "Now we have to do some rearranging to even things out."

She visits the overpopulated groups and asks people what books they've read in the past year, what their favorite movies are, and which TV shows they watch on a regular basis. People start migrating to other groups, some good-naturedly, others looking seriously disgruntled.

Robby sits grinning at me the whole time. I study

him discreetly, noting his thick black hair and bright, brown-eyed gaze. He's wearing jeans and a maroon T-shirt that says "Big Deal," whatever that means. This morning in homeroom, Mr. Paulson introduced him as Roberto, but he'd barely gotten the *to* in Roberto out when Robby cut in, saying he'd prefer to be called Robby.

Finally the groups are established. The Romance and Horror groups each have six people, while the other two groups have five. Robby and I have picked up Ashley Elizabeth, who got ousted from Romance, and identical twins Kevin and Kenny Faidley from West End.

The twins don't say much. They're tall and gangly, with unruly red hair that makes them look a little bit like roosters. They're wearing faded blue jeans and plaid shirts that match, except that Kenny's is green and Kevin's is blue. Maybe that's to help people tell them apart.

"This is so unfair," Ash says, slouching in her chair with her arms folded across her designer chest. "I mean, big deal, so I used to read Nancy Drew books. It's not like I've read all of them. And I didn't even like them that much," she says loudly in Miss Chappell's direction. Miss Chappell is laughing with the Romance people and doesn't hear.

"Just give it a chance. It won't be that bad," says Robby.

Our first task is to come up with a mystery book to read in September. All the groups are supposed to pick a classic for the first month. We go over Miss Chappell's list of classic mystery novels and decide on *And Then There Were None* by Agatha Christie. Or, rather, Robby decides. He's the only one who does any talking. The rest of us just grunt and nod.

When the bell rings, I rush out the door. It's lunchtime, and I'm looking for Lindy. But Miss Chappell's room is at the far end of the building, and by the time I get to the cafeteria, the line is snaking out the door along with the zesty aroma of barbecue sauce. When I finally get inside and spot Lindy, she's sitting at a crowded table, laughing at the girl across from her.

I might be looking for Lindy, but she's not looking for me. Did she forget we were supposed to eat lunch together?

I saw her only once after she got back from vacation. She had an end-of-summer party at her house, but there were so many other kids there, I didn't even get a chance to talk to her.

I load my lunch tray with food I don't want and navigate to a table that still has a few empty seats. I think the people sitting there are eighth graders. They shoot me curious glances as I sit down and then go back to their conversation like they've already forgotten about me.

Oh, seventh grade is going to be a blast.

Chapter 11

"Can I sit here?"

I look up. Robby Morales is standing there, holding his lunch tray. He's waiting for my reply, like I have some say in where people can sit. I shrug indifferently, and he slides in next to me.

"I'm so glad they made barbecue chicken tenders the first day," he says. "I love barbecue chicken tenders. And it's great how you get to pick your side dish. We never got choices at my old school back in New Mexico."

I spear a single macaroni noodle with my fork and force it through my clenched teeth.

"So, where are you from?" asks Robby. "You're new, too, right?"

I lower my fork and send him a deadly look. "I've lived here all my life."

"Oh, sorry. I didn't think you knew anybody. I mean, I didn't see you talking to anybody."

"I guess I'm just not in a talkative mood," I mutter.

"That's okay. Everybody gets like that sometimes."

His gaze on me is intense. All morning, every time I looked up, that gaze was on me. Then he ended up in my reading group. Now here he is at my lunch table. Maybe the mall egging has me paranoid, but it feels almost like he's stalking me.

"Stalking you?" He sounds indignant. "I'm not

stalking you. I just thought we could be friends."

Oops. Did I actually say *stalking me* out loud?

I look him up and down. "And why would you want to be my friend?"

"I have to start somewhere. Maybe you do, too."

I think this over. And I remember how my mom and I made a sort of pact to stop pushing people away.

"Fine," I say with a sigh. "So how come you hate your name?"

He looks at me serenely. "I don't hate my name. I like my name. My parents named me after my grandpa back in Nicaragua."

"You told Mr. Paulson not to call you Roberto."

He shrugs. "If my name was William, I'd want to be called Will. If it was Jacob, I'd go by Jake. It's like that. I mean, if your name was—I don't know—Cassandra, wouldn't you want your friends to call you—"

"Chloe—hi."

I whirl around, and there's Lindy, on her way to the trash can with her lunch tray. I notice right away that her shoes are very different from mine. She's wearing metallic gold flats, whereas I'm in black sneakers.

"Hey, Lindy," I say, aiming for nonchalance.

"I looked for you," she says feebly. "I couldn't find you. So I sat with some people from my class."

"It took me a while to get here," I tell her. "I have English class right before lunch."

"English class! That's so far away. Hey, what do you think about Miss Chappell? She's pretty awesome, isn't she?"

"Pretty awesome," I echo.

"Well, see you." She flashes a quick, bright smile and hurries away. I notice that she didn't say anything about trying to meet up for lunch tomorrow. She didn't offer to save me a seat at her table. She rejoins her seven-two friends at the big trash can near the door, and they chatter a mile a minute as they dump their lunch trays.

As I watch her walk out of the cafeteria, I know that she's also walking out of my life.

"Who was that?" asks Robby.

"Nobody important." I spear three macaroni noodles and shove them into my mouth. "Just somebody I used to know."

Chapter 12

I hate getting up early, so it's a blessed relief when Saturday morning rolls around and I get to sleep in.

Then I wake up and find out there's been another egging.

Mom tells me about it at lunchtime. This time Maynard's Shoes was the victim. A bunch of shoes on display out front got hit. Like last time, the police think the crime took place in the middle of the night.

"How many—" I begin.

"Eight. They used eight eggs."

We eye each other uneasily. Outside the living room window, a lady says contemptuously, "She acts like she's the first woman on earth to ever have a baby."

Mom turns abruptly and heads into the kitchen. I'm right behind her. We park ourselves in front of the refrigerator.

"I bought a new carton on Thursday," she says, twisting her opal ring around and around on her pinkie. "I haven't used any eggs at all. If you haven't either, there should still be a full dozen."

"I haven't used any," I tell her.

She takes a deep breath and tugs open the refrigerator door. She has the grim demeanor of a fourteenth-century villager about to open a vampire's coffin. She takes out the egg carton and places it on the counter. Gingerly, she lifts the lid.

There are four eggs inside, crowded together at the left end of the carton. The rest of the carton looks starkly empty, like eight tiny bird's nests emptied of occupants.

"Oh!" Mom clamps a hand over her mouth. "How can this be?"

I can only stare at the carton in silence, dazed by the undeniable truth. Somebody is taking our eggs and using them to attack mall stores. I just don't know who or how or why.

Mom is looking desperately at me. "Did you drop the carton and maybe break some? It's okay—I won't be mad."

"I haven't touched the carton."

She paces around the kitchen, taking short, quick steps because it's a tiny room. "I don't understand. What's going on?"

"Somebody's stealing our eggs," I say, and that impossible truth sounds even more impossible spoken aloud. "Did you lock all the doors and windows last night? Did you bolt the doors?"

"Of course. Do you still double-check them before you go to bed?"

"Always." It's something we're both paranoid about. The mall is a creepy place at night when nobody's around. "Were the doors still bolted this morning when you got up?"

She nods.

"Maybe the person came down the chimney," I say. "Like some kind of evil Santa Claus."

She takes a moment to think that over. "That would be difficult, to say the least. Going back up would be even harder. And it doesn't explain how they got into the mall after hours. Besides, why would somebody break into our house just to steal eggs? If they're going to go to all the trouble of breaking in, why not steal our computer or my jewelry, or—or—" She gestures toward a jar on the kitchen counter. "—the grocery money?"

Mom always makes sure there's cash on hand in case I need to run to Shop and Save. The jar is in plain sight. I can see the green bills curled inside, two twenties and a ten.

She's staring at me expectantly, waiting for more theories about how eight eggs just walked out of our refrigerator. But I'm out of ideas.

"That's it. No more eggs for us," my mother says fiercely. "I'm just not going to buy them anymore. If we want eggs, we'll go out to breakfast."

"Fine by me," I say.

She pulls out a chair and plops down at the table. "Jack Caldwell will be saying we're the prime suspects again. After all, we had opportunity."

"But not motive," I say, sitting down across from her. "Maynard's Shoes isn't your rival. You don't sell shoes." I gnaw at a jagged edge of my thumbnail. "This has happened twice now. Don't you think we should tell the police?"

"No!" she says immediately. Then, with a sigh, "I don't know. Maybe."

"Look, it's not like we're guilty," I remind her. "We'll just tell the truth and let the police figure things out. That's what they do."

A group of teenage girls giggle outside the kitchen window. A relentlessly crying baby goes by. A lady says, “Whatever happened with that friend of yours who found the nest of opossums in her sock drawer?”

Mom is hunched over the table. She says, in a thin voice, “I’m just afraid if the police find out how much you hate living here, they’ll think you’re the one doing the eggings. To get us evicted.”

I’m so flabbergasted, I’m speechless. For a few seconds, anyway. “I can’t believe you would even say that! You think I’m doing the eggings?”

“Not me. But the police might.”

“Oh, so now you’re playing devil’s advocate. Like Jack Caldwell.”

I know what “playing devil’s advocate” means because I looked it up after Jack said it, after Ram tried to say it. It means “taking the opposing viewpoint for the sake of argument.”

“I’m just trying to think like the police. Trying to consider all the possibilities.”

“Oh, yeah?” I stand up, shoving my chair away. “Well, I know I didn’t do the eggings, and you said nobody could have broken into our house. So that leaves you. You must be the guilty party. How’s that for a possibility?”

And I stomp through the living room and storm out the front door.

I realize almost at once that leaving my house was a bad idea, though my pride won’t let me go back. When I’m mad, I just want to be alone in a quiet place, which is the opposite of what the mall offers. And today there’s so much movement, so much noise. Shoppers shopping. Salesclerks selling. Music blaring. People laughing. That yippy little stuffed dog doing somersaults in front of the toy store.

I push through the milling shoppers, impatient with their dawdling, hating them for their cheerfulness. I bet they wouldn't be so happy if they had to live here.

I pass a rack of discounted ladies' tops in neon colors so bright that they leave an afterimage when I look away, like when you glance at the sun. Watches and necklaces and rings in a jewelry store window catch the light from different angles, twinkling like lightning bugs as I walk past. I wish I had my sunglasses.

Eventually I end up in Farringer's, my favorite department store. The department I like best is Ladies' Wear because it goes on and on for miles, like a forest. In fact, when I was eight or nine, that's exactly what it was. The endless racks of clothing were lush, bright trees. The price tags were slumbering butterflies. I'd spend long summer afternoons hiking deep into the woods, letting the fabrics brush my skin like summertime leaves and inhaling that new-clothes smell like it was fresh air.

Once I found a hollowed-out tree trunk that was actually a circular rack of long dresses. I burrowed inside and curled up on the cushy carpeting, and it was so cozy I fell asleep. When I finally woke up and burst out of those dresses, I scared some lady half to death.

Today, just like in the old days, I go weaving around the clothing racks crammed with shirts and skirts and blouses and dresses and slacks and suits, and even some winter coats, though it's only late August. Deeper into the woods I go until I'm so hopelessly lost I'll probably never be found. And that's fine with me.

I'm thinking about eggs the whole time, but I never come up with any answers.

Chapter 13

"I have exciting news," says Miss Chappell. "There's going to be a school-wide contest. It's called Creative Endeavors, and it's for writers, poets, artists, and photographers. As Accelerated English students, you should all think about entering one of the creative writing categories."

"Do we get money if we win?" asks Leonard Borowski.

"As a matter of fact, yes," Miss Chappell says joyfully. "There will be a small monetary prize for first, second, and third place in each category."

"Then I'm entering every category!" declares Leonard. "I need the money."

A few people snicker. Ash tosses her head, letting everybody know *she* doesn't need the money.

Tara Leibowitz raises her hand. "Does school-wide mean we'll be going up against eighth and ninth graders? Because that doesn't seem fair."

"No, no," says Miss Chappell. "Each grade will have its own separate contest. Sorry for not making that clear. You'll be competing only against other seventh-graders."

She glances around the classroom to see if there are any other questions and then continues. "The official flyer will be coming out tomorrow, so you'll find out all the details then. But start thinking about what sorts of projects you might want to enter."

At lunchtime Robby tells me he's thinking about entering the Creative Endeavors contest.

"Are you a writer?" I ask. I'm soaking my grilled cheese sandwich in my tomato soup, trying to drown out the plastic taste of the cheese.

"Photographer. Kind of. Trying to be. How about you? Are you going to enter?"

"No."

You'd think somebody whose mother owned a craft store would be at least a little bit artsy. But I don't draw or paint or whittle wood or do any of the other things artists do. I don't own a camera. I've never written a story except when forced to by some teacher, and even then my work hasn't exactly gotten rave reviews. I hope Miss Chappell won't be disappointed that I'm not entering.

"You've been kind of quiet lately," Robby says. "Quieter than usual, I mean."

I shrug.

"There's a word for that kind of quiet," Robby goes on. "But I can't remember what it is. Wait, I know. Preoccupied. That's how you seem—preoccupied. Like there's something you can't stop thinking about."

I give him a long, thoughtful look. Every day he feels less like That Pesky Stalker Guy and more like a friend. We've started to share things. Facts about ourselves. Feelings. Our likes and dislikes, although those exchanges are lopsided, because Robby doesn't seem to have any dislikes. He's a half-full kind of guy, somebody who can see the good in any situation. This seems like a good way to be, yet I sometimes find it annoying.

"You're right." I sigh. "I am preoccupied." And then I tell him about the Oasis Mall eggings and how our eggs keep going missing.

"Wow," says Robby when I've finished. "You're so lucky. First, you get to live at the mall—"

"I hate living at the mall," I growl.

"—and now you have a real, live mystery, just like in the books we're reading."

I stare at him darkly. "Lucky? It doesn't feel that way to me."

"Hey, maybe I could help you solve the case. How about if I come home with you after school today? Maybe your Shadow Vandal left some clues."

I raise an eyebrow. "Shadow Vandal?"

"Yeah." Robby adopts the hushed, melodramatic tone of a movie-trailer narrator. "He lurks in the shadows with his basket of eggs, waiting for nightfall so he can do his evil deed. Watch out, mall dwellers—it's the Shadow Vandal!"

He grins at me. I stare back soberly, refusing to be humored. "You won't find any clues. Everything's all cleaned up and back to normal."

"Well… They say criminals always return to the scene of the crime. We can conduct surveillance, check people out. See if anybody looks suspicious."

"If you want to," I say indifferently. But I'm thinking how nice it will be to walk around the mall with a friend.

Chapter 14

Robby rides the school bus home with me. You're supposed to get permission from both sets of parents and the school office before taking a different bus, but we don't bother with all that. Robby keeps his head down as he gets on the bus, and the driver never notices him. Robby's parents won't be home from work until after six, so he has plenty of time to catch the mass transit bus back to his neighborhood.

We drop our book bags on the living room floor. I give Robby a tour of our house—living room, kitchen, bedrooms, bathroom.

On our way back to the kitchen, I hear a click behind me and whirl around to see Robby opening the cellar door.

"Whoops!" I say. "Could you shut that door, please?"

"You didn't tell me you had a cellar."

I give him a deadpan look. "Hey, Robby—I have a cellar. Now shut the door."

"Aren't we going to go down there?"

"Why would we?"

"So I can check it out. It's the only part of the house you haven't shown me."

"Trust me, you don't want to see the cellar. It's icky down there."

"I don't mind icky."

"Well, I do. Now shut the door, and let's get something to drink."

"How about if I go down by myself? It'll only take—"

Before he can finish, I've reached around him and slammed the door shut.

He gives me a mock-wounded look. "Sheesh. You hiding a dead body down there, Mall Girl?"

"Five dead bodies, actually. Look, I just don't want—" I stop, narrowing my eyes at him. "What did you call me?"

"Mall Girl." He grins. "Do you like it? It just came to me. I think I'll call you that from now on."

"Fine," I say airily. "Then I guess I'll call you Roberto."

He just laughs.

In the kitchen I pour us each a glass of iced tea, and we sit at the table, talking about school. After a while, Robby says, "What's that clinking noise I keep hearing?"

So I tell him about the fireplace coins. Robby runs to the living room to see for himself, and when a nickel comes ping-ponging down the chimney, he lets out a whoop of joy and claps his hands like he's just observed a dazzling magic trick.

"We give the money to charity," I tell him, "every year at Christmastime. This year it'll be an animal shelter. Last year it was a children's hospital. Mom lets me keep some for myself as payment for packaging up all those coins and taking them to the bank. She calls me the Coin Management Officer."

After we finish our drinks, we head out into the mall and find a bench near Maynard's Shoes. We sit there watching people go by—elderly couples inching along arm in arm, merry clusters of teenagers. Mothers pushing babies in strollers trailed by sulky six-year-olds. Solitary old men with slouchy socks and sad eyes. Nobody looks suspicious. I'm not even sure what suspicious looks like, but Robby says we'll know it when we see it.

After a while we head to Greetings, and since Connie's Cupboard is right next door, I take Robby in to meet my mother.

Robby shakes my mother's hand, and Mom beams so hard over my new friend, she practically gives him a sunburn. She invites him to stay for dinner, but Robby declines politely, saying he has to be home by six.

"Maybe we're going about this all wrong," says Robby as we hang around outside Greetings. "The Shadow Vandal is probably planning his next attack. He wouldn't be visiting the stores he already egged."

So we walk through the mall, turning our heads this way and that way as we search for somebody who looks crafty and malicious, somebody who's eying up stores in a casing-the-joint kind of way. We have plenty of time to look around because we're creeping along at a turtle's pace. I'd prefer to go faster, but there's no room to pass the endless clump of shoppers in front of us. We're stuck in place, like riders on a carousel.

While we're upstairs, Robby insists on making a wish on my chimney. He throws four pennies, finally getting the last one in.

"Score four cents for the animal shelter!" he crows. But he won't tell me what he wished for.

We make another lap around the upper level, though our enthusiasm is starting to wane. Nobody looks like a vandal.

"It'll probably turn out to be the last person we'd suspect," I say, eying a sweet-faced old lady the size of a nine-year-old.

Robby doesn't respond, and when I glance over my shoulder, I see him twenty feet back, peering in the window of Royal Jewelers. I backtrack, pushing my way through oncoming shoppers until I reach him. He's gazing at a double-strand diamond necklace that costs eight thousand dollars.

"My birthday's not till January," I tell him. "But if you start saving now, maybe you'll have enough by then."

He flashes a quirky grin but doesn't explain why he's looking at a necklace that's worth more than my mother's car.

"Hey," he says, "you want to go get some ice cream at the food court?"

Robby orders a mint-chocolate-chip cone, while I opt for a hot fudge sundae. We pick a table near the edge of the food court so we can continue to observe shoppers passing by. But our hearts are no longer in the surveillance operation.

"This place smells so good," says Robby. He sucks the pointy-swirly top off his ice cream, his eyes roving across the assortment of food places bordering the seating area. "All those different smells are making me want more than just ice cream."

"That's the idea," I tell him. "The food court restaurants blow their kitchen fans out into the mall so people smell the good smells and go over to buy something."

At the moment, the orangish-brown aroma of taco

meat fills my nostrils. A minute ago, it was the curry-heavy scent of Indian food. The smells keep changing, depending on which way the air is moving.

"It's working," says Robby. "I just might have to grab a slice of pizza for the bus ride home."

"Uh-oh." I slide down in my seat. "Don't look now, but here comes Ash."

"Ashley Elizabeth?" He cranes his head around. "Where?"

"Never mind. She just got on the escalator. She's with Tara Leibowitz. Luckily, she didn't see us. Not that she would have said hi or anything."

He turns to look at me. "How come you don't like Ashley Elizabeth?" There's no judgment in his gaze, just curiosity.

"Because she's Ashley Elizabeth!" I say, rolling my eyes. As an afterthought I add, "Don't tell me you like her."

Robby takes two quick licks of his ice cream. "I think a lot of people have the wrong idea about Ashley Elizabeth. I talk to her after school a lot because we both ride late buses. She's nice."

"Whoa. You're kidding, right?" I give him a sideways, sarcastic look. "Oh, wait. I almost forgot—you're a guy. All the guys like Ash, right? Ash, with her flirty white smile and her designer clothes and—and that hair."

Robby gazes at me placidly. "I like your hair better. It's so yellow. And your curls are really pretty."

I make a scornful *puh* sound. "I hate my curls!"

"Why? Curly hair is so much more interesting than straight hair."

"Interesting? Try tangly, messy, hard to control."

Robby shifts in his chair. “Okay. Then why don’t you do something about it?”

“Huh?”

“If you hate your curly hair so much, why don’t you straighten it? That’s what my sister does. She buys the stuff at the drug store.”

That suggestion leaves me stunned. As often as I’ve cursed my curly hair, I never considered taking steps to straighten it.

“Well. Maybe I will,” I say.

I dig my plastic spoon into my sundae, making sure to scoop up a bit of everything—ice cream, fudge sauce, whipped cream, nuts. I shovel the spoon into my mouth, savoring the way the ingredients swirl together in a luscious clash of opposites. Warm collides with cold, salty with sweet, crunchy with silky smooth.

I glance around at the nearby food court patrons. Sitting cattycornered from us is a little family—a mom, a grandma, and a tiny baby girl in a stroller. All three of them are wearing T-shirts with sayings on them. The baby’s shirt, a hot-pink thing with lace at the neck, has the words “Just Hatched” above a decal of a wide-eyed yellow chick busting out of an egg. The mom’s shirt says “Super Wife, Super Mom, Super Tired.” The grandmother’s says “World’s Best Grandma.”

Watching the baby wave her tiny arms, I think about how she’s going to grow up, how someday she’ll be the one wearing the “World’s Best Grandma” shirt. Then I think about all the T shirts she’ll wear in between. Shirts advertising her favorite cartoon character, the name of her school, the rock star she’s dying to meet. Shirts that broadcast the clubs she belongs to, the places she’s visited.

It occurs to me that you could sum up somebody's whole life in T-shirts. In my mind I see all the sayings from all the shirts a person ever owned, typed up on a single sheet of paper, like a poem.

"Oh!" I say.

"What?" says Robby.

"Nothing. Ice cream brain freeze." This idea is too new to share, even with Robby.

I wasn't planning to enter the Creative Endeavors contest, but I think maybe there's a poem in me. I gaze out into the mall, pretending to scan the crowd for the Shadow Vandal. But what I'm really doing is observing the sayings on peoples' chests.

Drama Queen

Jesus Loves You

Recycling: It WORKS

Virginia Beach is for lovers

Don't give me ATTITUDE I've got my own

My mind and my heart race as I imagine the finished product. I'll use different font sizes and styles and colors. Print it on some kind of fancy paper.

I can hardly wait to get started.

Chapter 15

Crawford Heights Junior High School proudly announces the first annual Creative Endeavors Contest.

Do you have a unique voice? A fresh way of seeing the world? Do you write poetry or short stories? Do you like to paint or draw? Take pictures? Make movies? If so, Creative Endeavors is the contest for YOU. Let your creativity EXPLODE. We encourage unusual forms and new approaches.

Deadline for Entries: September 30

Prizes per Category/Grade:

First Place - $25

Second Place - $15

Third Place - $10

Categories:

Creative Writing/Short Story

Creative Writing/Poetry

Art /Painting

Art/Drawing

Photography

Short Video

Join us for the Creative Endeavors Awards Ceremony on October 15 at 1 p.m. in the school auditorium.

****

I grab a Creative Endeavors Contest flyer from the table in the school foyer. I keep bumping into people in the hall because I'm reading the flyer as I walk.

"Unusual forms and new approaches," I muse. That seems to describe my poem.

Heartened, I flip the page over and skim the contest rules, which tell what the word limits are for the various written works, how short the short video should be, and what sort of subject matter would be deemed inappropriate. The judges for the creative writing categories will be a college English professor, an English teacher from a neighboring school district, and a newspaper editor.

I get to English class a little earlier than usual. Hardly anybody is in the room. Ash is up front talking to Josie from the Romance group. They're speculating about which has a better chance of winning the Creative Endeavors contest—a rhyming poem or a non-rhyming poem. In the end, they just don't know. I hear Ash say, "Well, I guess I'll enter some of each and see what happens."

Great. I'm going to be competing against Ash. Ever since she got second place in a countywide essay contest back in fourth grade, everybody's thought of her as the Class Writer. Nobody more so than Ash herself.

Kenny and Kevin arrive and nod their hellos. A minute later, Ash slides into her seat and assumes her usual arms-crossed, why-do-I-have-to-be-here posture. Robby steps through the door just as the bell rings.

Miss Chappell tells us to go ahead and start discussing our books. Today we're focusing on plot, talking about what's happened so far and speculating about what might happen next.

Robby leans toward me. "Hey. Mall Girl. I have a

new theory about your mystery. I'll tell you at lunchtime."

He says it softly, but because we're sitting at desks pushed together, everybody in our little group hears.

"You have a mystery?" says Kenny, perking up. "You mean like a real one?"

"We're good at solving mysteries," Kevin adds. "Over the summer our grandpa thought the neighbor's dog was pooping in his yard. We figured out it was a skunk."

"We set up a motion-activated video camera," Kenny continues. "Caught the critter in the act."

"It was coming into his yard every night to do its business."

The twins have a pent-up way about them, like wind-up toys that somebody cranked the whole way up and then turned off. They're quiet most of the time, but once they start talking, it's like, pow! They spring loose.

"Really?" says Robby. "So how'd your grandpa keep the skunk from pooping in his yard?"

"He didn't," says Kenny.

"But at least he stopped blaming the neighbor's dog," says Kevin.

"So, what's the big mystery?" asks a sardonic voice. We all glance over at Ash. Although she dutifully participates in our book discussions, she's never shown the slightest interest in our personal conversations.

"Yeah, Chloe." Kevin seconds the motion with a wave of his hand. "I'd like to hear about it."

I'm a private person. I don't tell my business to just anybody. But here I am, in a group of people who like mysteries, who have read lots of mystery books—or, in Ash's case, not-so-many Nancy Drew books. Maybe they've absorbed what they've read. Maybe they've learned to think like detectives. Maybe, just maybe, one of them will come up with an idea Robby and I haven't thought of.

So I tell them about the Shadow Vandal. I even call him that because I've gotten to like the name. It makes him sound glamorous, like somebody Batman would tangle with.

Kevin and Kenny stare at me intently as I talk, jiggling their knees. Ash is doodling hearts adorned with curlicues all over her tablet like I'm not captivating enough to warrant her full attention. Robby is sitting back with his arms crossed, letting everybody know my story is old news to him.

"So the police don't have any leads?" asks Kenny when I've finished.

"If they do, they're not saying."

"Has anything else in your house gone missing?" asks Kevin.

"Just the eggs."

"It doesn't make sense," Kenny says. "Why would this Shadow Vandal break into your house to steal your eggs? Wouldn't he bring his own?"

"Not if he wasn't planning to egg the mall," Kevin replies.

We all look at him.

"Maybe he decided to break in on the spur of the moment," he says. "The first time, anyway. Once he was in, he was like, 'Okay, now what?' And then he thought, 'Well, maybe I could egg a store.' Because he remembered how there's this whole house right there in the mall, which would probably have eggs in the fridge, so…"

"That still doesn't explain how he got into our house," I point out.

Ash puts down her pen and looks at Robby. "You said you have a new theory."

"Yeah." Robby squirms in his seat. "Chloe might not like this, but…I was thinking maybe her mom's the guilty party. Like, maybe she's been walking in her sleep."

"That's crazy!" I sputter. "My mother doesn't walk in her sleep."

"You think she did the eggings when she was awake?" asks Robby.

I glare at him. That's even crazier.

"It would explain some things," Kenny says. "Like how your doors are still bolted in the morning. She unbolts the door when she goes out and bolts it again when she comes back in."

I shake my head emphatically. "My mother is not the kind of person who would throw eggs. Ever. People don't do things when they're asleep that they wouldn't do when they're awake."

"That's hypnosis," Ash says. When we look at her quizzically, she goes on, "You're thinking of hypnosis. They say you can't make a person do something when they're hypnotized that they wouldn't ordinarily do."

"Yeah, I've heard that," says Robby.

"But is that true about sleepwalking, too?" Kevin asks. "Let's say you have some good, decent person who never broke the law in their life. Let's say they start sleepwalking. Could they commit a crime in their sleep?"

"And if they did, would they remember it?" adds Kenny.

"Or would it feel like a dream?" asks Kevin.

"Sleepwalking. Wow," says Miss Chappell, who has been standing nearby, listening in. "You guys are taking *And Then There Were None* in a whole new direction! Good for you. You're thinking outside the box."

We wait self-consciously for her to wander away.

"You know what I think?" says Ash, glancing from Kenny to Kevin to Robby but skipping me entirely. "I think Chloe's mom is innocent."

"Thanks, Ash," I say, surprised and a little touched that she's taking my side.

"I think Chloe's the one who's been walking in her sleep," Ash goes on. "I think she's the Shadow Vandal."

Chapter 16

I'm the Shadow Vandal.

I'm furious at Ash for suggesting it, though I know if she hadn't thought of it, one of the others would have.

Riding home on the school bus, I give the idea a few minutes of serious consideration before rejecting it completely. I am not a sleepwalker. If I was, there would be signs. Mom would hear me moving around, or I'd go to the kitchen to make a snack and forget to put the peanut butter away. Or I'd be really tired the next day. But none of those things have happened.

And I don't think Mom is a sleepwalker either, for the same reasons.

Which brings us back to square one. Back to the question no one can answer. Who took our eggs?

When I get home, I'm surprised to find the front door open. Voices drift from the kitchen, the voices of my mother and Ron Caldwell.

"...just not safe anymore," Ron is saying.

"Come on, Ron," says my mother. "We're not talking *Murders in the Rue Morgue* here. Some eggs got thrown, that's all. Jack's hired an extra guard for the night shift, so if the guy tries it again, there's a good chance he'll be caught."

"The climate in this mall is changing, Ursula. There's a downward spiral underway. I've seen it before. Things can go from bad to worse pretty quickly."

My mother sighs. "But if we moved downtown, we'd be in a different school district. Chloe would have to switch schools."

"All the more reason to move," Ron says smoothly. "Willowdale is one of the best school districts in the region. Much better than Crawford Heights. They don't do that scholastic grouping you hate so much. And if you compare the average grades on the standard achievement test—"

"I know you have our best interests at heart. But I don't want to move downtown. I'm sorry."

"Okay. All right. That's fine." I can't see Ron, but I imagine him putting his hands up in a placating gesture. "It was just a suggestion. Greg was my friend, and I've always felt I owed it to him to look out for you and Chloe. I just wonder what he would say about the situation."

"I think he'd say, 'Ursula, do what your heart tells you.' "

I choose this moment to bang the screen door. Abruptly, the conversation in the kitchen ceases. My mother comes into the living room, Ron right behind her.

"Oh, hi, Uncle Ron," I say.

"Hey, kiddo, how's it going?"

"Good. Mom, why aren't you at the store?"

"I'm taking a little break. I'm about to head back now. Thanks for coming by, Ron. You're a good friend." She gives his hand a squeeze.

I didn't realize moving downtown would involve switching schools. I'm surprised by how much I hate the idea. Despite my heartache over Lindy, I suddenly realize I like school this year. I like having Robby for a friend. I like all my classes and my teachers, especially Miss Chappell. And I'm excited about the Creative Endeavors contest.

After I change my clothes, I go out into the mall and sit on a bench near Deluca's Sporting Goods with a pen and notepad, conducting pre-poem research. I'm amazed by how many people tell the world about themselves through the messages on their chests.

I see shirts advertising food products, motorcycle brands, local companies, and vacation spots. Shirts proclaiming the best sports team. A couple of shirts with R-rated messages, worn mostly by college-age guys. And mom-shirts galore—*Best Mom on Earth, Mommy of 3, MOM is WOW turned upside down.* Being a mother seems to be something women are really proud of.

Within an hour, I have a whole page of T-shirt sayings. I head home to my computer, open a new word-processing document, and type *Life in T-shirts by Chloe Lamont.*

That's the easy part. Now I have to figure out which sayings to include. I pick out three that seem right and type them, double-spaced and center-aligned. First is *Just Hatched,* in honor of the food court baby, then *I [heart] Cats,* and *Trophy Wife*. I apply a fancy, hot-pink font to *Trophy Wife* and find a clip-art heart that I use for *I [heart] Cats.*

My poem is officially underway.

Chapter 17

On a Sunday morning in mid-September, I'm jolted awake by a shriek. "Chloe! Get in here!"

It's not the gentlest way to wake up, but in this case it's better than staying asleep, considering I was at the very beginning of the spider dream.

"Mom? What's wrong?" I stumble out into the hall.

Mom, in her bathrobe, is standing just inside the kitchen. She beckons me in and points to the floor. Our eight-inch carving knife is lying there, between the table and the refrigerator.

"Did you do that?" she asks.

I look at her blankly. "Do what?"

"Put that knife on the floor."

"Why would I put a knife on the floor?"

"Exactly," says Mom.

"Oh, no!" My heart seems to slide up into my throat. "You mean—"

"It wasn't there last night," she says in a tremulous voice. "I just got up, and when I came into the kitchen, there it was. Lying in the middle of the floor."

"Oh," I say in horror.

What has the Shadow Vandal done now? Murdered somebody? Apprehensively, I circle the knife, examining it from all angles. There's no blood. At least not on the side that's showing.

Mom's face is almost as white as her bathrobe.

"Are you sure you didn't use that knife last night? I know how you like to have sliced banana with dabs of peanut-butter for a snack."

"I had popcorn last night. Anyway, if I was going to slice bananas, I wouldn't use a big, sharp knife like that."

The doorbell rings. Mom and I both jump, and I kick the knife under the stove without even thinking about it. Mom sends me a look that's a mix of reproachful-grateful and hurries to get the door.

It's Ram. I breathe a sigh of relief to see him standing there unmurdered and then freeze as a police officer steps out from behind him. I recognize him as one of the policemen who were at the scene of the first egging. Officer Sanford, the burly one with the shrewd gaze.

"Ursula. Chloe. Can we come in?" says Ram, looking grim.

He tells us there's been another vandalism incident, this one involving a knife. The second he says knife, my knees go weak. I struggle to stiffen them, all the while trying to keep my expression serene.

The good news is, no one was murdered. The bad news is, some merchandise in kiosks got slashed to shreds. Although the permanent stores are protected by sturdy walls and steel security gates, the kiosks in the middle of the corridors have only flimsy curtains around them at night. The vandal slit open the curtains of three kiosks and proceeded to slash away. The victims, all at the Deluca's end, were Teddy Bear Den, Quality Handbags for Less, and Hats For All Occasions.

We're standing in our living room, Mom facing

Officer Sanford and me facing Ram, like two couples about to start square-dancing. Except if anybody tried to square-dance in our living room, they'd take one galloping step and crash into a wall. The room feels crowded and overwarm with four people in it. I'm having trouble breathing. I feel like Ram and the cop are sucking up all the air.

"I know you guys aren't close to the crime scene," Ram says, "but did either of you see or hear anything unusual last night? It would have been around one a.m."

"We were sleeping," says my mother.

Officer Sanford takes a step forward, showing that he, not Ram, is in charge here. "So you were both home last night? All night?"

Mom and I nod.

"Do you ever leave your house at night?" asks Officer Sanford. "Maybe just go walking around the mall?"

"Absolutely not," says my mother. "We're not allowed to do that. It says so in our contract."

"But surely there are times when you have to leave the mall or return home late at night. So you'd be walking through the mall at those times."

"Well, yes," my mother says. "But we don't have to walk far. The door we use is down that way—" She makes a fluttery gesture. "—past the main corridor. Near the mall office."

Officer Sanford scribbles on a notepad. "And how do you get in after hours? I assume the door is kept locked."

"We have a key." My mother is anxiously clenching and unclenching the dangling ends of her bathrobe belt. I mentally will her to stop, but the message doesn't get through.

"Just the one key?"

"Yes."

"Have you given a copy of it to anyone? Your parents, a boyfriend, anybody like that?"

"No. Nobody. We wouldn't be able to copy it even if we wanted to. It's a special kind of key that has to be ordered through the mall office."

Officer Sanford scribbles some more and then slips his pen and notepad into his pocket. "Here's what happened, ma'am. One of the guards says he was down near Deluca's last night when he spotted an intruder in the main corridor. The guard yelled, 'Stop,' but the person took off running. Darted toward the center of the mall. By the time the guard got to the Farringer's wing, nobody was in sight. Shortly afterward, he discovered the damage to the three kiosks."

I don't ask how long it took the guard to reach the Farringer's wing, but if it was Hal, the regular night guard, I guarantee he didn't break any speed records. Hal is the most out-of-shape person I've ever met. Even when he's in a hurry, he can't manage much more than a lumbering saunter, the kind of pace a person might set while touring an art museum.

My mother is frowning. "Around one a.m., you say?"

"Yes, ma'am. Did you see or hear anything out of the ordinary around that time?"

"No. Chloe and I never hear much of anything at night. We run air purifiers in our rooms." She gives a nervous laugh. "You know, to filter out all this stale mall air. The purifiers do the job, but they're pretty noisy."

"How about you?" Officer Sanford says to me. "Did you see or hear anything unusual?"

"I was asleep, too." I hate the way my voice trembles.

"The whole time? You didn't leave your house after your mother went to bed?"

"No."

He's studying me intently, his eyes narrowed like he's trying to peer into my very brain. But when he speaks, his tone is light, as if we're just having a friendly chat. "Seems like living here could get boring for a young person. Especially at night, when you have to stay in your house. I'll bet a lot of kids would sneak out after their parents went to bed. Just for something different to do."

From the corner of my eye I see my mother make a jerking movement. I know she wants to lash out at Officer Sanford because of what he's getting at, but she doesn't dare.

"I never do that," I say evenly. "Ever."

Officer Sanford's eyes are still locked on mine, as steely as handcuffs. I force myself to stare back. I want him to see the innocence in my eyes, but I don't think he can. I think he thinks I'm the vandal.

Finally, he looks away. He gives a curt nod. "Well, thank you, ma'am. Miss. We may have more questions later."

After they leave, we just stand in the living room. I'm looking at my mother, but she won't look back.

I say, "Maybe we should tell—"

"No." She cuts me off abruptly. "There's no reason to. This knife thing? It's nothing. In fact, I think I know what happened. I swept the kitchen floor last night. The knife was probably under the table, and I swept it out to the middle of the floor without even noticing it."

I think that over. "How could you sweep a big knife like that across the floor without noticing it?"

"Easily, that's how. It was late. I was tired."

"But how did the knife get under the table in the first place?"

Now she turns her eyes on me, and I'm startled and hurt by the coldness I see there. "One of us dropped it, obviously. We are done talking about this. Understand?"

Later, when she's in the shower, I use a spatula to slide the knife out from under the stove. A bunch of other stuff comes with it—uncooked spaghetti noodles, a withered baby carrot, mini dust bunnies. I pick up the knife and study it carefully.

Stuck on the tip is a tiny piece of fuzz that may or may not be a bit of teddy bear stuffing.

Chapter 18

T-shirt sayings have taken over my life. They're everywhere—jotted on torn-out sheets of notebook paper, scribbled on sticky notes, scrawled on the jacket of my math book, and written in fading ink on the back of my hand.

Now I have to narrow them down, pick the best ones. Although there are dozens, I take the time to write each saying on a separate index card. That way I can sort them into categories, move them around like chess pieces, and select and reject them with ease.

It occurs to me that I'm not just building a poem—I'm creating a character. Who is this person wearing all the shirts? Where does she like to go? What does she want to be when she grows up? Imagining her as an actual person makes it easier for me to pick the right sayings.

On a whim, I change *Just Hatched* to *Daddy's Baby Girl*, because I think that's what I was when I was very small. I send my girl to nursery school, and later she joins a pee wee soccer league.

She'll need hobbies and activities as she grows up. A favorite sport. Should she be a cheerleader? No. A skateboarder? No. A dancer? No again. How about a basketball player? A swimmer? A skier? Yes—a skier! I flip through my index cards and place *I'd Rather Be Skiing* off to one side.

She goes to college (*University of Maryland*) and takes a trip to the beach (*Virginia Beach is for lovers*), where she meets her future spouse (*Trophy Wife*).

Next I pull out all the job-related index cards. I had to search the Internet for job sayings because I didn't find enough on T-shirts. Maybe people aren't as gushy about their jobs as they are about other things in their lives.

I read the job cards one by one.

Old accountants don't die—they just lose their balance.

Teachers Have Class.

Nurses Call the Shots.

Waitress Extraordinaire.

Librarians do it by the book.

That last one sounds a little bit dirty, so I rip up that card. I don't want to get disqualified for being inappropriate. I consider a few more contenders and then decide on the nurse saying.

Skier, college student, nurse, wife. T-shirt Girl is beginning to plump out, like a balloon filling with air. She's becoming real.

Chapter 19

One day in late September, I come home from school to find a railroad track encircling my house. Two workers are in my yard, fiddling with a kiddie-sized train. It consists of two open cars, a caboose, and a shiny red and black engine.

"Now what?" I say with a sigh, stepping across the track.

"Hey! Kid! Get off that track!" One of the workers, a chubby guy with spiky blond hair, starts striding toward me.

"Hey yourself! I live here!" I yell back. I dart up the porch steps and into the house before he can say anything else.

When my mother comes home, Ron is with her.

"…gone too far this time, that cousin of mine," Ron is saying as they barge in through the front door. "Hi, Chloe. You can't let him get away with this, Ursula."

I slap my book shut and stand up. "Mom, what is going on?"

"Halloween, that's what." She flops down on the couch. "Jack decided the mall needed a train for little kids to ride. Apparently, all the malls put them up at Halloween, and this is the only wing wide enough for it to fit."

"Ursula, we can fight this," says Ron, sitting next

to my mother. “Jack may be my cousin, but family bonds only go so far. Especially since he’s being such a jerk. I’ll help you—you know I will.”

“We can’t beat Jack,” my mother says wearily. “We can dispute this, we can sue him, but by the time a hearing gets scheduled, Halloween will have come and gone, and the train will be history.”

Ron sighs like he knows she’s right.

“Well, then,” I say, “we’ll just have to remember to look both ways before crossing the train track.’

My mother laughs softly. “Right. So we don’t get hit by a pint-sized train going two miles an hour. Right outside our house! It’s so absurd, it’s comical.”

“Jack is trying to make life difficult for you,” Ron says. “He wants you out of his mall. The novelty of the Oasis Mall Family has worn off, so he’s not gaining a thing by having you here. In fact, you’re costing him money. If you weren’t here, he could put half a dozen kiosks where your house is now. Collect thousands of dollars more in rent every month.”

“Don’t you think I know he wants us out? That’s exactly why I’m determined to stay. Here’s what we’re going to do.”

Mom’s plan is to decorate our yard for Halloween like it’s never been decorated before. She wants to send Jack Caldwell the message that the train doesn’t bother us in the least. In fact, we think it’s great.

“Let’s give the little kids something fun to look at,” my mother says. “It’s not their fault Jack Caldwell is a jerk.”

The three of us go shopping, and we buy so many decorations, we have to borrow a cart to bring them home. We turn our yard into a spooky wonderland.

There are plastic vampires, inflated giant jack-o-lanterns, ghosts and bats and gravestones. A Frankenstein monster whose eyes light up green. A motion-activated witch that cackles when the train goes by.

Take that, Jack Caldwell.

Chapter 20

My poem is finally finished. At least I think it is. I sit on my bed, reading it over and over. It's good, but I keep getting the feeling there's something more to be done.

I read it again. Suddenly the title, "Life in T-shirts," doesn't seem quite right. It's not just life—it's a particular person's life.

I should give her a name, this fictitious T-shirt wearer of mine. The name should be part of the title—*Somebody's* T-shirts. Kylie comes to mind. That's what I'm planning to name my first-born daughter.

"Kylie's T-shirts." I say it out loud several times to test the sound of it. I write it on a piece of paper to see how it looks.

No. Kylie is a young name. It works for a ten-year-old, a twenty-year-old, maybe even a thirty-year-old, but not for somebody pushing ninety.

I rack my brain for older names. Esther, Susan, Dorothy. Now I have the opposite problem. They're good great-grandma names but don't work for a tiny baby.

I think and think and finally come up with Sarah. It's a classic name, one that can take a person from brand-new baby to old, old lady.

And at last my poem is complete.

Sarah's T-shirts

by Chloe Lamont

~~*

Daddy's Baby Girl

I'm the Big Sister

Starshine Nursery School

Linville Pee Wee Soccer League

I (heart) Cats

I'd Rather Be Skiing

Born to Drive

Middleford High School Debate Team

University of Maryland

Nurses Call the Shots

Virginia Beach is for Lovers

I'm with HIM

Trophy Wife

Baby on Board

Super Mom, Super Wife, Super Tired

PROUD PARENT of a Springville Middle School Honor Student

My Son Went to Miami and All I Got Was This Stupid Shirt

Have you hugged a vegetarian today?

OVER THE HILL

Got troubles? Call 1-800-GRANDMA

Retired and Loving It

I got pills to improve my memory, if only I could remember to take them

World's Greatest Great-Grandma

As I finish reading, I get another idea. I'll print my poem on T-shirt-shaped paper. This will make it stand out as an "unusual form."

I figure I can make my own special paper, a T-shirt being such a basic shape. My first attempt is terrible.

The paper T-shirt comes out as lopsided as a real shirt that's been stretched in different directions after years of wear. Then I think of drawing half a T-shirt on folded paper and cutting it out, the same way you'd make a paper heart. That works great. The symmetry is perfect, though it takes a few tries before I get the proportions right.

Finally, I have it. My poem, centered on a T-shirt-shaped sheet of paper. But because the T-shirt paper is smaller than standard size paper, I'm worried that it will get lost among the other contest entries. I need to glue it to something larger, like colored construction paper.

I don't have construction paper, but I find an eleven- by fourteen-inch piece of white poster board stashed behind my dresser. White is all wrong, of course—the white T-shirt shape wouldn't stand out—but I can fix that by coloring the poster board. There's a can of hot-pink spray paint in the cellar that will work just fine.

Now I just have to work up the nerve to go fetch it.

Our cellar has always creeped me out, though I don't know why. Maybe because it's underground, like a dungeon, and the only way out is up the stairs. Maybe I've watched too many movies about subterranean monsters.

It's a partial cellar, which means it has even less space than the first floor, and it's divided into four small rooms. At the bottom of the stairs is the family room, which has thin, stained carpeting and old-fashioned furniture from when my dad's parents were young. There's also a furnace room, which features an area with shelving and a counter where my grandpa used to work on carpentry projects. Next to the furnace room is a cramped bathroom that includes a tiny shower splotched with ancient black mildew. Last is the laundry room. All the walls have flimsy, fake-wood paneling, a look that apparently was all the rage in the 1970s.

I open the cellar door and stand braced in the doorjamb, like a diver about to plunge into icy water. Then, before I can get myself too worked up, I go charging down the stairs. I race to the laundry room, grab the can of spray paint from the shelf above the washer, and race back upstairs, slamming the door behind me. It takes a minute for my heart to settle down.

Mom used the spray paint earlier in the summer to give new life to an old, dark-wood picture frame that's now hanging on my bedroom wall, framing a picture of three kittens. Hot-pink is perfect for my girlie T-shirt theme.

I know Mom would not want me using spray paint in the kitchen, but there's no way I'm doing it in the cellar. And I'm not about to do it outside, in view of passing shoppers. I get a stack of old newspapers from the hall closet and use them to paper the entire kitchen floor. The ancient linoleum is as ugly as can be. It's yellowish-tan, though I think it started out white. It's cracked in a bunch of places and curling up at the edges. In my opinion, some hot-pink accents would be just the thing to perk it up, but I don't think Mom would agree.

While the poster board dries, I clean up the kitchen. I place the can of spray paint just inside the cellar door, on the top step, telling myself I'll take it back to the laundry room later. Deep down, though, I know that won't happen. Mom will nag me for a while and then take it down herself. I fold up all the newspapers, many of which are now adorned with random pink splotches, like modern art, and stuff them in the kitchen waste basket.

Mom gets home around ten. She had a good day at work. She makes popcorn and tells some funny work stories, and we laugh together. I tell her about the contest and let her read my poem, and she really likes it and is excited for me. Things seem to be back to normal, though I know they're not really. Our problems haven't gone away. They're lurking just below the surface, like a slumbering subterranean monster.

Chapter 21

"So I'm getting my entry ready for the photography contest," Robby says at lunch. "Tell me what you think." He reaches into his book bag and pulls out several sheets of notebook paper with photos taped loosely to them. "This isn't the finished thing. It's just to give you an idea."

Robby is calling his entry "Alike." It's a series of photographs of things that resemble one another, though you might never notice the similarities if Robby wasn't there to point them out.

First there's a photo of a distant highway at dusk. Two lanes of cars are streaming down a curved stretch of highway. The headlights are slightly blurred, creating a twinkling effect. The opposite lanes of the highway aren't visible, so you don't see any red taillights. Just the shining white-gold headlights.

Next to the headlight photo is a close-up photo of a double-strand diamond necklace on a gray cloth. The necklace is curving in the same direction as the highway, and the sparkling diamonds look like glowing headlights.

Who would have thought a diamond necklace could resemble a congested highway? Only Robby.

"I took the picture of the headlights when we were on our way here from New Mexico," Robby tells me. "We were staying at a motel with this far-off view, and

I could see headlights coming down a highway. I thought they looked really pretty. Later I saw the diamond necklace at the mall."

"That day you were there with me!" I say.

"Yeah. That necklace reminded me of the headlight photo. And that's when I got the idea for the contest. Later I went back and asked the jeweler guy if I could take a picture of the necklace. He said yes. He even found me a gray cloth to lay it on."

"This is awesome," I murmur, my eyes flicking back and forth between the two pictures.

The next photo shows a cat's face superimposed on the front of a car. The cat's slanted eyes are perfectly aligned with the tilted headlights, so it looks like the car is turning into a cat, or vice versa.

There are several more photos—a piece of broccoli that looks like a fallen tree, a lady with the face of an ostrich, a rock formation that resembles a man slouching over a golf club. I think of how the Creative Endeavors flyer said "Do you have a fresh way of seeing the world?" and I think that in Robby's case the answer is yes.

"Your entry is really great," I tell Robby, handing back the papers. "Guess what? I've decided to enter, too."

I have a folded draft of the poem in my purse. I smooth it out and hand it to Robby, explaining how and where I got the idea and how the actual contest entry is on T-shirt-shaped paper glued to pink poster board.

"This is amazing," he says, his eyes roving down the page. "My grandparents are always talking about how fast life goes by. Your poem shows that. But it's also about how good life can be. It's like a mix of happy and sad. And the T-shirt-shaped paper? That's just brilliant."

"Thanks." I'm flushed all over, warmed by his praise. "I'm glad you like it."

"It's weird that we got our ideas the same day, huh?" He hands my poem back with a grin. "See? The mall isn't so bad after all. It's a great place to get ideas."

I start to roll my eyes, like I usually do when somebody uses the word *great* to describe the mall. But then I stop myself and nod instead, because in this case I think he's right.

****

The next morning—the day of the contest deadline—I take my poem to the school office to hand it in.

The secretary says, "Okaaaay," in a dubious voice as she glances pointedly at a shallow cardboard box labeled "Poetry—Seventh Grade" that's partially filled with nice, orderly eight-and-a-half-by-eleven-inch sheets of paper. My eleven-by-fourteen piece of poster board doesn't fit, so she has to lay it across the top of the box.

As I leave the office, I feel a great sense of relief. It's over. No more laboring over my poem, making changes, second-guessing myself, wondering if it's the best it can be.

The winners won't be announced until the awards ceremony on October 15, so there's nothing to do now but wait.

Chapter 22

We're on our third mystery book. Miss Chappell wants each group to do some kind of class presentation in December about one of the books we've read. Or all the books we've read. Or something related to our reading group in some way. She's being deliberately vague because she wants the ideas to come from us. She's all about creativity, Miss Chappell is. In fact, I have a feeling she was behind the Creative Endeavors contest, because people have said that it never existed before this year.

Robby says there's a movie version of *And Then There Were None*. He suggests we get together to watch it. Comparing the movie with the book might be a good approach for our presentation. We can have snacks, turn it into a party.

So we start talking about where and when, and Kenny nominates my house.

"Sure," I say. "I'll have to check with my mom, but I'm sure it'll be fine."

We plan tentatively for the last Saturday in October. What better time to watch a mystery movie than Halloween?

"I don't know if I can make it," Ash says, tossing her hair around like she's too good to hang out with us. "I have an ice skating lesson that day."

"So get out of it," Kenny says severely. "This is a

class assignment. You have to be there."

Ash crosses her arms and glowers at him.

****

On the day of the awards ceremony I'm so nervous I barely touch my lunch, even though we're having pizza, one of the few dishes the cafeteria manages to get right. In the auditorium Robby and I sit propped together like two halves of an arch.

I remind myself that if I don't win any prizes, at least I won't be publicly humiliated. Robby is the only person from school who knows I've entered, and he's promised to keep it a secret.

Mr. Zimmer, the principal, walks onto the stage and welcomes everyone to the Creative Endeavors Awards Ceremony. The winning pieces will be posted to the school website by the end of the day. Seventh grade is up first. We'll be starting with the art categories, then moving on to video, photography, poetry, and short story.

Pictures of the winning art pieces are projected onto a screen as the winners walk across the stage to receive their prizes. In Art/Painting, first place and second place go to West Enders. In Art/Drawing, an East Ender, Chad Bartlett, claims the top prize, which isn't surprising. He's been the best artist in our class since kindergarten. But West Enders take second and third. This makes me wonder if maybe West End has a better art program than East End.

Miles Lawrence, another West Ender, wins short video. Mr. Zimmer gets his name wrong and calls him Lawrence Miles, a problem the poor kid has probably had all his life.

Miles' film is hilarious. It's called "It Came in

With the Laundry," and it's a spoof of 1950s creature features. It's about this small, hairy monster—a Halloween wig, actually—that crawls out of a hole in the ground into a woman's laundry basket and proceeds to terrorize her family. The film is really clever, and the special effects are amazing for a seventh grader.

We move on to photography. I hear Robby draw in his breath, and I pat his arm. Third place is announced. It's not Robby. Second place is announced. Roberto Morales! I'm disappointed he didn't get first place, but Robby doesn't seem to mind. He pumps a fist into the air, grinning elatedly.

"Congratulations!" I say when he returns to his seat with his prize envelope. I'm curious to see the entry that beat his. It had better be good.

Turns out it is.

The winning photo was submitted by Kane Nakamura, who sits cattycornered in front of me in Miss Chappell's class. Kane's photo shows our school at sunset, and I think it just might be the prettiest photograph I've ever seen.

The last sliver of sun is peeping up over the school's roof, its orange rays reaching up and out like fiery spokes. The sky is a swirl of color—oranges and reds tinting the horizon, pinks and purples lighting up the ruffly clouds overhead. The school, bathed in a gauzy pink-purple glow, looks like a fairytale castle minus the turrets. The wide green lawn out front is slightly blurred, giving it a velvety look.

"Wow," says Robby, the word coming out on a long, slow breath. "That photo is, like, perfect. The lighting, the composition, the colors. I can never get my sunset pictures to come out right. I keep trying, though.

And I'm saving up to buy a better camera."

I tap his prize envelope with my forefinger. "Well, now you're fifteen dollars closer."

My anxiety level shoots sky-high when Mr. Zimmer announces the poetry category. Since the poems are so short, all the winning entries will be read aloud.

Ash is in the row in front of me, three seats to the right. She's leaning forward, her posture as rigid as an exclamation point.

She entered three poems and a short story in the contest, and she seems to think she has a good chance of winning at least one prize, and probably four. Not that she's come out and said so. It's all in her demeanor, the way she's been tossing her hair around anytime someone mentions the contest.

I think my poem is good, too, but I'm not sure I'll win anything. It's not just about how good my poem is—it's how good it is compared with all the other poems. Yesterday Miss Chappell read the statistics on the contest entries. Fifty-seven poems were submitted by seventh graders.

That's a whole lot of competition.

Mr. Zimmer announces the third-place winner. It's Carlie McIntosh, a seven-one West Ender who's in the Romance reading group. Carlie, a perpetually grinning girl with wavy, short brown hair, reads her poem.

Dead Roses
by Carlie McIntosh
~*~

It wasn't any earlier
Than just last week, I think,
That I looked out my window

And saw the roses, pink.

~*~

The blooming, blushing beauties
Smiled up at the blue sky,
So plump and soft and full of life,
Their fluffy heads held high.

~*~

They quivered in the summer breeze,
Their scent perfumed the air.
You'd never dream two weeks before
The buds weren't even there.

~*~

But now the pink is turning brown,
The blossoms drop their heads.
It's time for them to fade away,
Their petals crushed and dead.

~*~

Now that they're gone, I realize
I didn't take time to see
The special beauty of the roses
Sent from God to me.

~*~

I looked just once to note the blooms
And then they slipped my mind.
I didn't take time to really see—
How could I be so blind?

Wow. Carlie's poem is good. Suddenly I'm worrying about my own poem. Is it poemish enough? What if it got disqualified for being too big for the box? Would somebody have told me, or would they have tossed it in the trash and forgotten about it?

I glance over at Ash. She looks worried, too.

"Second prize," says Mr. Zimmer, "goes to Prisha

Khatri for her poem 'Music.' "

Prisha is from West End, but I don't know which section she's in. She's tall and dark-skinned, with extremely good posture, like somebody in the army. Mr. Zimmer hands her the prize envelope, and Prisha agrees to read her poem.

Music

by Prisha Khatri

~*~

Music throbs sweetly in my head,

tingling my senses into new awarenesses.

Music flows over and through me,

melting away into the dark corners of my being.

Music caresses the invisible substance of my soul,

awakening long-hidden, bittersweet memories from their slumber.

Music glistens in the shadows behind my eyes

and whispers to me of timeless dreams.

Wow again. These West Enders are good poets.

"And our first place winner," Mr. Zimmer says grandly, "in the seventh-grade poetry category. Chloe Lamont, for her poem 'Sarah's T-shirts.' "

Robby jumps up and down, whooping into my ear. I slide past four people in my row and hobble to the stage, hoping my shaky knees don't give out before I get there. This moment seems unreal.

Somehow I manage to read my poem. When I return to my seat clutching the envelope containing my twenty-five-dollar check, I don't even look at Ash. She's probably shooting poison arrows through my head, but it doesn't bother me—because I won!

And though she entered three poems and a short story, Ash doesn't win any prizes at all.

Chapter 23

The next morning, Mom and I find out there's been another incident. And by morning, I mean two-fifteen a.m.

Despite our noisy air purifiers, the pounding on the front door wakes us both. We stagger to the living room in our pajamas and bathrobes, exchanging looks of dread. We know even before Mom unbolts the door what this is about.

Hal is standing on our porch, huffing and puffing like maybe he had to up his usual walking pace from leisurely saunter to moderate stroll.

"It's happened again," he says, panting. "Another attack. I was down by the doughnut shop when Tom, the other guard, calls down to me from the upper level. 'Intruder!' he says. Hoo, let me catch my breath."

He clutches his heaving chest for a minute and then continues. "Anyway, I saw the guy maybe fifty feet away. I yelled for him to stop, but he took off. Turned down the Farringer's wing. When I got down here—nothing. Not a soul in sight."

Hal stares at us meaningfully.

"Well, where do you think he went, Hal?" my mother asks in her scratchy pre-breakfast voice.

"He couldn'ta gone nowhere, Ursula. That's the thing. All the stores got their gates in place. There aren't any exits in this wing. The only place he coulda gone is right here. Into your house."

I gasp and step closer to my mother, glancing around the living room, then toward the kitchen. An intruder in our house? It's a notion out of a thriller movie.

My mother is shaking her head. "There's no way he could have gotten into our house. The door was bolted just now when I came into the living room."

"What about the back door?" I say.

My mother whirls around and marches toward the rear of the house. I'm right on her heels. Hal, not bothering to wait for an invitation, enters the house and follows us.

The back door is bolted, too.

We check the windows. All are locked. Hal keeps barking importantly into his walkie-talkie, communicating with Tom. He says things like "roger that" and "perpetrator" and "oh-two-hundred hours," trying to sound like actual law enforcement and not just a night guard in a shopping mall. He tells us the police are on their way.

"What kind of attack?" my mother finally asks.

"He used spray paint this time. Vandalized about five stores between Deluca's and the Farringer's wing."

Spray paint! I'm on the verge of swooning. I almost ask if the spray paint was hot pink but stop myself in time.

"So it was a man?" says my mother. "You keep saying 'he.' "

"I don't know if it was a man. Gotta call him something. Ain't about to keep saying 'he or she.' The person wasn't very big—I can tell you that." His eyes drift to me.

We pace around the tiny living room as we wait for the police. Finally there's a rap on the door. Two police officers are standing there—Officer Sanford, the burly, shrewd-eyed cop who interrogated us after the knife attack, and Officer Pritts, the sandy-haired younger cop who looks like a veterinarian. Officer Pritts smiles at me. Officer Sanford does not. *Good cop, bad cop,* I think.

Officer Sanford tells Hal he's wanted at the scene of the crime, where several other police officers are gathering evidence. Hal gives my mother and me an uncomfortable nod and ambles away.

Officer Sanford asks the usual questions. Where were we tonight, did we see or hear anything unusual, did we leave our house at any time after mall hours, did we give anybody a key.

Then he asks my mother, "Do either you or your daughter own a dark-colored hooded sweatshirt?"

My mother looks at him in bewilderment. "Hooded sweatshirt? What does that have to do with—? Oh! Is that what the vandal was wearing?"

"Ma'am, if you could just answer the question."

She nods impatiently. "Of course we own sweatshirts. Who doesn't?"

"What colors?" Officer Sanford persists.

"Mine is white," says my mother.

Officer Sanford turns his stern gaze on me.

"Orange, navy blue, and maroon," I say. "That's three separate sweatshirts," I clarify. "Not just one. Because a sweatshirt with all those colors in it would be plain ugly."

"We'll need to see them," says Officer Sanford, scrawling notes on his pad. "Not the white one. Just the others." He looks at my mother. "Do you have any spray paint in the house? Pink spray paint, in particular?"

I feel a hot flush creep up the back of my neck and wonder if I'm going to pass out. I try to keep my breathing slow and steady, but it's a real struggle.

I can almost hear a click as Mom's armadillo shell slides into place. "Spray paint? Are you kidding me? Do you actually think we did this? Is that what you're saying?"

"Ma'am, please. We're trying to conduct an investigation."

Even though Officer Sanford is asking the questions, Officer Pritts is the one Mom looks at. "I don't know. It's possible. I can't be sure."

"Okay," Officer Sanford says, shoving his notepad and pen into a pocket. "We need to take a look around. You can let us do that now, or we can get a search warrant."

Search warrant! That's what the cops on crime shows get when they think they've found the guilty party and want to search his house.

"By all means, look around," Mom says. "We have nothing to—hide."

She falters on that last word, like maybe she just remembered the spray paint can. She knows I left it on the top cellar step. The can isn't noticeable when you go down the stairs because it's nestled in the corner of the step. But every time she comes up from the cellar, she spots it and says, "Chloe, the next time you go to the cellar, please take that can of spray paint down."

Since I never go to the cellar, the can hasn't made it back to the laundry room. It's possible the Shadow

Vandal took the can with him when he was done vandalizing those stores. But if he put it back on the cellar step, the officers are going to find it.

"Okay, then," says Officer Sanford. "Let's get started."

Chapter 24

Officer Pritts goes through the coat closet, while Officer Sanford gropes beneath couch cushions and peeks under furniture. Then Officer Sanford moves to the fireplace, drops to his hands and knees, and peers up the chimney. If it was later in the day, there'd be a good chance a coin would ping him on the head.

We move into the kitchen. The search there takes a while because we have so much stuff crammed into our cabinets. Dishes, pots and pans, food items, cleaning supplies. The officers even look in the refrigerator. And the oven. And the trash.

Then Officer Sanford eyes the cellar door and asks, "Does that go to the basement?"

My mother nods mutely. My heart is pounding so hard, my entire body feels like a huge, pulsating organ.

The officers follow my mother down the stairs without noticing the can. A crazy idea pops into my mind. As soon as they disappear into the cellar, I'll grab the can of spray paint and hide it in the oven. They've already searched the kitchen, so they won't be looking there again.

But when Officer Pritts reaches the bottom step, he pauses and looks up at me. "You coming?" he asks with a kind smile. He still doesn't seem to notice the spray paint can.

Numbly, I plod down the steps. Halfway down, I

glance back up the stairs.

The can of spray paint isn't there.

I look around discreetly as our little group moves through the cellar. There's no sign of the spray paint can anywhere. When we get to the laundry room, I see that it's not on the shelf above the washer either. Did the Shadow Vandal take it with him? Or did he leave it someplace else in the house?

Between my worries about the paint can and my cellar phobia, which is only slightly lessened by the presence of police officers, my anxiety level is halfway to the moon. The officers take their good old time as they poke around. I clamp my lips together to keep from screaming.

Officer Sanford tries the door to the furnace room and turns impatiently to my mother when he finds it locked. My mother shows him where the key is—hanging on a nail beside the door, concealed behind an old bureau. She explains that we keep the door locked out of habit. When I was little, my grandpa had a workshop in there. The grownups wanted to make sure I didn't wander inside and hurt myself on his tools.

There isn't much in the furnace room, so the search only takes a minute. Even so, I shiver convulsively the whole time Officer Sanford is in there, more on edge than ever. I breathe a sigh of relief when he comes out and locks the door behind him.

We troop back up to the kitchen and then head to the rear of the house, where the two bedrooms are. The officers search Mom's room first. They peer under the bed, open her closet door, and go through her dresser drawers. The whole thing is humiliating, especially the part where Officer Sanford roots through her underwear drawer. Mom stands with her arms crossed in front of her, staring at the floor the whole time.

Officer Pritts searches the bathroom, which doesn't take long. Then they head into my room.

I hold my breath, waiting for them to zero in on the kitten picture hanging above my desk, the one in the hot-pink frame. Mom spray-painted that frame with the very same paint that's gone missing, the paint that was obviously used in the attacks. But their sharp cop gazes go flitting right past, probably because so many other things in my room are pink—my bedspread, my curtains, a furry foot-shaped throw rug next to my bed.

Officer Pritts pulls a banana out of my sock drawer and shoots me a quizzical look. I look away, defiantly silent. Let him wonder. I am in no mood to explain the theory of banana separation.

Officer Sanford spreads my three sweatshirts out on my bed and bends over to examine them, first the fronts, then the backs. I assume he's looking for telltale splotches of pink spray paint. When he's done, he gathers them up in a clump and hands them back to me, stony-faced.

Finally the search of the house is done. We watch through Mom's bedroom window as the officers search the back yard, which takes a while because of all the Halloween decorations. Then they examine the train, car by car. Finally they leave.

"Go back to bed," my mother says. She won't look at me, and that hurts more than Officer Sanford's accusing stare. I know what's going on in her mind. It's not that she thinks I did it. She's just not sure I didn't.

"I don't feel good," I say. "Can I stay home from school?"

"Yes." She turns toward me and plants a kiss on my forehead. Her lips are so cool they send a chill through me.

Chapter 25

I go back to bed but don't get back to sleep for hours, and even then it's a restless, unsatisfying sleep haunted by half-dreams about handcuffs and jail cells. The police didn't find the spray paint can, but the poster board my poem is mounted on is the same shade as the paint used in the attacks. What if somebody at school makes the connection?

I get up for good around noon and eat food I'm not hungry for. I open a book I can't concentrate on. I keep thinking back to how happy I was yesterday when I won the contest, how my mother literally jumped up and down when I told her. How we went out to eat at Mama Rosa's to celebrate and things were good between us. It's not fair that one of the best days of my life has to be followed by one of the worst.

And just when I think things can't get any worse, they do.

A little before four o'clock, Robby calls.

"So, are you actually sick?" he asks. "Or did you skip school today because you heard about the poetry thing?"

My heart does an odd little bobble. "What poetry thing?"

Robby tells me that Ash and her parents are contesting the results of the poetry competition—specifically, the fact that I won. Mr. Hutzell read my poem on the school website, and he's saying it should have been disqualified because it isn't something I wrote myself. All I did was compile sayings created by other people.

"He's just mad because Ashley Elizabeth didn't win any prizes," Robby says. "He probably figures that if you get disqualified, they'll bump the second-place winner up to first place and third place to second, and then maybe Ashley Elizabeth will get third."

"Can he do that?" I ask in dismay. "Make the school disqualify my poem? Just because he wanted his own kid to win a prize?"

"He can't make anybody do anything. Miss Chappell says the school board will hear both sides and make a decision. They'll do that at their meeting on Thursday."

"So they might take my prize away."

"That won't happen," Robby assures me. "Miss Chappell told me the judges are going to go to the school board meeting and tell why they picked your poem. Don't worry—everything will be fine."

But the way my life has been going lately, I'm not so sure.

My mother is furious when I tell her about the poem situation. "The Hutzells, huh? That figures. People like that kill me, the way they think they can bully the world into giving them whatever they want. Well, it's not going to work this time. When is that school board meeting? We're definitely going."

"You're not going to stand up and yell at people, are you?" I ask apprehensively.

"Not if I don't have to," she replies, which I don't find reassuring.

When bedtime rolls around, I'm wide awake as can be, my mind racing with dark imaginings. What if the school board sides with the Hutzells and takes my prize away? What if the police find the spray paint can, with my fingerprints on it, and arrest me? What if Robby drops me like a hot potato because he doesn't want to be friends with a criminal? What if my mother adopts an orphan from Romania to fill the void in her heart after I get sent to jail? What if she forgets all about me?

What if the whole world forgets about me?

Chapter 26

The room where the school board meetings are held is packed. People are standing two deep along the back wall because there aren't enough seats. One guy is fanning himself with his baseball cap, another with a dog-eared pamphlet. I wonder if the meetings are always this crowded or if more people than usual showed up because of the poetry contest dispute. I guess if you weren't directly involved, it could be entertaining, almost like a sporting event.

Ash and her parents are sitting to the left, near the front of the room. Ash sees us come in and immediately looks away. She's been ignoring me all week at school and was conveniently absent from English class on both Tuesday and Thursday, the days of the regular reading group meetings.

The second- and third-place winners, Prisha and Carlie, are here with their parents, too. Carlie doesn't see me, but Prisha does. She waves and shoots me a half-hearted smile. I understand why they're here. If my poem gets disqualified, Prisha and Carlie will each move up a place. I wonder if they're rooting for Ash.

The seven members of the school board are sitting at a long table at the front of the room, facing the audience. First they have to take care of some run-of-the-mill school board business. They discuss possible changes to the school visitors policy and vote to buy new ninth-grade history books. There's talk of renovating the gymnasium next summer. Then it's our turn.

The school board president, a bald man named Mr. Dougherty, briefly explains the situation and then invites Ash's father to speak.

Mr. Hutzell strides to the front of the room and adjusts the microphone stand so it's taller. He starts out by saying that to his way of thinking, a poem should actually be written by the person who's claiming it as her own work. But all I did was copy T-shirt sayings onto a piece of paper and turn it in as a poem. And, as ludicrous as it sounds, I won!

I can feel heat coming from my mother, like she's literally smoldering. I lean my head against her shoulder, trying to calm her. I'm praying she won't jump up and start yelling.

Mr. Hutzell goes on to tell how his daughter, who is a very talented writer and in fact got second place in a countywide essay contest in fourth grade, wrote three beautiful poems all by herself and yet won no prize at all. He's always told his daughter that justice will prevail in the end, but it's very hard to convince her when situations like this arise. He implores the school board to disqualify my poem.

Miss Chappell gets up to speak next. She looks like an underfed teenager with her toothpick legs sticking out below the hem of her black leather miniskirt. But when she speaks, she's every bit the confident, grown-up teacher.

She explains how she came up with the idea for the Creative Endeavors contest and stresses that the word "creative" in the name is key. She passes out contest flyers to the school board members, telling them to note the highlighted sentence “We encourage unusual forms and new approaches.” My poem is just one example of the unusual forms that were submitted.

Then she gives each member a stapled handout containing the three winning poems. She also reads each poem aloud for the benefit of the audience. She has my actual contest entry there, and she holds it up so everybody can see how I printed the poem on T-shirt-shaped paper. She points out that my poem is a visual piece as well as a textual one.

Two of the three contest judges are here—Dr. Margaret Pelesky, a distinguished-looking university professor, and Angela Sheehan, a seventh-grade English teacher at Willowdale Junior High. Miss Chappell tells the school board that the judges will explain how they came to choose my poem as the winner.

Mrs. Sheehan speaks first. “I think it is absolutely fitting that this poem won first place. And, yes, it is indeed a poem—one that required a great deal of creative thought.”

She smiles down at the paper in her hand. “I think it’s fascinating how this young writer created a character from T-shirt sayings. In a very few words, we learn all sorts of things about this character. She’s a beloved daughter, a big sister, a soccer player. Later she becomes a wife, a mother, a grandmother, even a great-grandma. She loves cats. She’s a nurse, a vegetarian, a skier. She was on her high school debate team. And all those facts are conveyed via T-shirt sayings.”

Next it’s Dr. Pelesky’s turn. She puts on her glasses and peers down at my poem, an expression of disdain on her aging face. That expression worries me until I realize it's her natural look.

"There is great poignancy in this piece," she says in a resonant, warbly voice. "It comments on life's brevity, on its preciousness, in a most original way."

I nod thoughtfully, trying to show that *poignancy* and *brevity* and *preciousness* were exactly what I had in mind when I created my "piece," though I'm not totally sure what *poignancy* means. I'll look it up when I get home.

"I stand by my decision," Dr. Pelesky goes on briskly. "This poem is unique. It's fresh. It is the hands-down winner. And if you decide anything other than that, justice will not have prevailed."

"This is the most preposterous…" Mr. Hutzell says loudly.

The school board members talk quietly among themselves for a few minutes. Then Mr. Dougherty asks if Chloe Lamont is present. My heart seems to stop. Are they going to want me to talk? Right here, in front of everybody?

"Stand up!" my mother whispers, so I do.

"Hello there, Chloe," Mr. Dougherty says with a kind smile. "Don't be nervous. We'd like to ask you a few questions. You can answer from where you are. Just speak up, okay?"

He asks how my poem came to be, so I tell him about the little family in the food court and how they made me start thinking about all the different T-shirts a person wears over a lifetime. I tell him how I collected dozens of T-shirt sayings and how it took weeks to shape my poem, to get a feel for the character it represented. To pick the most fitting sayings and arrange them in just the right order. To select the perfect font styles and colors. And to get my poem printed perfectly on my homemade T-shirt-shaped paper.

"Thank you, Chloe," says Mr. Dougherty. "You may sit down. All right, members—shall we vote? All in favor of declaring 'Sarah's T-shirts' by Chloe Lamont the official first-place winner of the seventh-grade Creative Endeavors poetry contest, say 'aye.' "

"Aye," murmur all seven members of the school board.

"Those opposed?"

Silence.

"All right. Chloe Lamont is the winner," declares Mr. Dougherty. "Congratulations, Chloe. Next on the agenda—"

"Hold on," calls Ash's father. He bumps past all the knees in his row and strides to the front of the room. His face is very red, and a three-dimensional vein is inching across his temple like a crooked worm.

Ash has slunk so low in her seat, a casual observer might mistake her for a pile of coats.

"Mr. Hutzell, your business here is concluded," Mr. Dougherty says firmly, but Ash's dad ignores him. He's beckoning Dr. Pelesky to the front of the room.

"Dr. Pelesky, would you mind?"

Wearily, Dr. Pelesky gets to her feet and hobbles forward. "What is it, Mr. Hutzell?"

Mr. Hutzell reaches inside his suit coat and pulls out a folded piece of paper. "This is one of the poems my daughter entered in the contest. I'd like you to read it. I want to know exactly what you think. Because it's very clear to me that Ashley Elizabeth deserved to win a prize. Her poem is much better than that dead flower thing that got third place."

Across the room, Carlie and her parents make outraged noises. Mr. McIntosh half-rises out of his seat, all clenched fists and murderous stare. Mrs. McIntosh tugs pleadingly at his sleeve, and he sits back down.

"I don't understand," says Dr. Pelesky, peering at Mr. Hutzell over the top of her glasses. "You want me to publicly critique your daughter's poem? What's to be gained? The contest is over. The winners have been chosen."

"Please," says Mr. Hutzell. "Read my daughter's poem. I want to know exactly what's wrong with it. I want to know why she didn't win a prize."

Dr. Pelesky looks toward the school board. Mr. Dougherty makes a sweeping go-ahead gesture. Mr. Hutzell hands the poem to Dr. Pelesky and then struts back to his seat. Dr. Pelesky clears her throat and begins to read Ash's poem.

Autumn Blues

by Ashley Elizabeth Hutzell

~*~

Most people are happy that autumn is here.

They welcome the idea that winter is near.

They anxiously wait for the cold, soggy snow

And tell the warm weather to hurry and go.

~*~

But me, I am different, I cherish the sun,

The sweet, tall, green meadows through which I can run.

I live for the summer when everything's warm.

I hate chilly autumn, then winter's dead form.

~*~

How I miss the blue sky with its clouds of white fluff.

It is now garbed in gray, looking gloomy and gruff.

Oh, the soft, friendly swish of the wind in the trees

Is now a cold villain that's making me freeze.

~*~

I dislike the short day and the long, chilly night.

I prefer the gold sun shining long, hot, and bright.

No more swimming, no picnics in the shade of a tree.

The cool, gloomy weather has murdered my glee.

~*~

Some people are happy that summer is gone,

But my memory of summer will live on and on.

Some people like coldness, in winter they thrive.

But the dream of next summer is what keeps me alive.

Dr. Pelesky has finished the oral reading, but she stands there for another minute, her lips moving. I figure she's giving it a second, silent reading.

"Well," she finally says, "I have to say that this poem has a consistent rhythm and a good rhyming scheme. Some of the lines are quite lovely. 'How I miss the blue sky with its clouds of white fluff. It is now garbed in gray, looking gloomy and gruff.' Very nice. The poet shows promise."

Across the aisle from me, Ash plumps up in her seat, her cheeks pinkening hopefully.

"However," Dr. Pelesky continues, her eyes sweeping down the page. "Overall, this poem doesn't stand out. Sun and run, thrive and alive—these are the most obvious of rhymes. And both the subject matter and the language are disappointingly ordinary. Poetry at its finest should be about expressing interesting ideas in unique ways. This poem doesn't deliver. Had we expanded the range of awards, it might have received sixth place at best."

I hear a little gasp and look over to see Ash burying her face in her hands. Her mother pats her back consolingly. Her father's face is a purplish hue that looks good on an eggplant but doesn't seem healthy for a grown man. He rises, grabs Ash's arm, and yanks her out of her seat so hard she stumbles. Mrs. Hutzell follows, her honey-brown hair flopping against her back as she walks. The three of them file out through the back, slamming the door behind them.

It's crazy, but I actually feel sorry for Ash.

After the meeting, people keep coming up to me and my mother to congratulate us. Miss Chappell scurries over to give me a hug and tell my mother what a wonderful student I am. My mother thanks her for all her help tonight.

Suddenly I'm face to face with Carlie McIntosh and Prisha Khatri.

"I'm really glad it turned out this way," says Carlie. "You totally deserved to win."

"Totally," says Prisha. "Your poem is awesome."

"Thanks, you guys," I say. "I think your poems are awesome, too."

"We're trying to start a poetry club," says Prisha. "Do you think you might want to join? Miss Chappell said she'd be our advisor."

Carlie adds, "But we have to have at least fifteen members for it to be an official school club."

My mother is standing there not saying anything, but her thoughts are coming in loud and clear. *You always push people away. Do not push these girls away.*

So I say, "Sure, I'll join," though I'm wondering how much I'll be able to contribute, considering I'm not even a real poet.

I guess I'll worry about that later.

Chapter 27

It's Saturday, the day of the Mystery Group movie event. I wake up with a groan, dreading Ash's visit to my house. Things are tense between us, to say the least, though we've established a kind of truce for Mystery Group.

I think Ash is having a tough time of it. She's been really quiet lately—even her hair seems subdued. Some people are against her because of what she did. They're calling her a sore loser. I could very easily join them. I could rub her nose in the fact that I won—twice, actually—and she lost. But I'm not going to.

I think there are certain situations in life that force you to decide what kind of person you are. Mean Girl is not who I want to be.

Mom and I spend the morning cleaning. Vanessa is running the store, which means Mom can stay home all day. But if I know my mother, she'll pop down to the store a couple of times to check on things. She can't help herself.

As I'm wiping off the kitchen countertop, I accidentally knock the outgoing mail to the floor. I pick up the scattered envelopes and sort through them, idly curious. Most are small and rectangular with preprinted business addresses showing through little plastic windows. Bill payments.

One envelope is different. Large, square, and

lavender, it's clearly a greeting card. I'm startled to see that it's hand-addressed to my mother. What's it doing in the outgoing mail pile? Then I notice the message scrawled across the front in Mom's handwriting. *Return to Sender.* She never even opened it.

Huh?

The return-address label tells me the card is from Doug and Laura Trimpey, and they live in Tampa, Florida.

Trimpey. That was my mother's name before she got married. Mom's birthday is a few days away. Could this be a birthday card from her evil parents? But if they're as evil as she says, why are they even bothering to send a card? And why is she sending it back unopened? Isn't she at least a little bit curious?

Impulsively I tear open the envelope.

Just as I suspected, it's a birthday card. On the front, above a vivid blue-green drawing of planet Earth, is the message, "To a Daughter Who Means the World to Us."

When I open the card, a hundred-dollar bill slips out. Inside there's a sappy little rhyming poem, like something Ash would write. Below it, in neat, right-slanting handwriting, is a more personal message.

"Happy Birthday, Ursula. We miss you so much! Won't you ever forgive us? We know we were wrong, but we only wanted the best for you. Still do. Please give Chloe our love. We are dying to meet her. Hope you're both safe and well. Love You Always, Mom and Dad."

I feel light-headed with emotion. I am flabbergasted, hurt, sad, furious—and determined to get to the bottom of things.

I slip the card back into its envelope and march into the living room. “What’s this?”

“What’s what?” Mom looks up from her dusting.

“This!” I wave the card in front of her face. “Your parents send you a beautiful birthday card, and you’re sending it back without even looking at it?”

Her face tightens. “You opened my mail?”

“Somebody had to,” I yell. “This is a birthday card from your parents. A loving message from the people who brought you into the world.”

“Chloe—” She looks away. “You don’t understand.”

“You said they were evil. They’re not evil. They love you. Why can’t you forgive them for whatever they did?”

She folds her dust rag into neat quarters and places it on the end table. “It’s not that simple. Years ago, we had this big falling out—”

“Over what? What did they do that was so terrible?”

“Okay, well, for starters, they didn’t like your dad. They didn’t even go to his funeral.”

That stops me. “Oh. Well, that wasn’t very nice.”

She fidgets a little, shifting from foot to foot. “Okay. In fairness—” She takes a breath. “—in fairness, they didn’t exactly know he had died. They’d moved to Florida by then. They didn’t find out until they started getting sympathy cards from friends who lived back here.”

“Wait a minute. You didn’t tell your parents your husband died?” I shake my head incredulously. “Then how could you be mad at them for not going to the funeral?”

She sighs. "I was just mad, period. And very distraught about your dad's death."

"But why didn't you tell them?"

She stares down at the ancient area rug, scuffing at a stain as if she can buff it out with her foot. "I didn't want them at the funeral. We weren't on speaking terms—and hadn't been since your dad and I got married. They didn't want me marrying him."

I think that over. "Well, even if that's true, it's not how they feel now. It says so right here in this card. They're saying they were wrong, and they're asking you to forgive them. Oh, and it also says they're dying."

I throw that last bit in for dramatic effect, to see if it will get a rise out of Mom. She doesn't disappoint.

"What?" She snatches the card out of my hand, fumbles it open, and scans the message inside. Then she gives me a wrathful look.

"They're not dying—they're dying to meet you."

"Oh, is that what it says?" I say innocently. I add, "Actually, I'd like to meet them, too. They're the only grandparents I have. I'd kind of like to have them in my life."

She hands the card back. "They live in Florida. They're too far away to be in your life."

"Seriously, Mom? Have you never heard of e-mail? Social media? Phone calls? Video chats?"

But she won't give in. "Too much time has passed. We're strangers."

"Mom," I say, waving the card at her again. "These people are reaching out to you. Do not push them away."

She just stares at me, throwing daggers with her

eyes.

"They're not just your family," I say. "They're mine, too. I have a right to know them."

But that's the last thing I get to say. My mother pivots on her heel and switches on the vacuum cleaner, and the T-Rex roar of it drowns out my very thoughts. Her message is clear—*conversation over.*

Chapter 28

As I'm getting dressed for the movie event, Mom steps into my bedroom. She tosses a blank manila envelope onto my bed.

"What's that?" I ask warily.

She bows her head. "You're right. It's my feud, not yours. Do what you want with these."

Then she's gone.

I reach into the manila envelope—gingerly, like there's something inside that could bite me—and pull out a small stack of sealed envelopes. Twelve, to be exact. Their size and shape tell me they're greeting cards. About half the envelopes are white. The others are a variety of pastel shades—pink, blue, yellow, green. Some have colorful stickers on them—smiley faces, birthday cakes, American flags.

I feel a flush of warmth when I see that they're all addressed to me and they're from Doug and Laura Trimpey of Tampa, Florida. I take a closer look. The postmarks tell me they were all sent around my birthday, one per year, beginning when I was a year old.

I flip through them one by one like I'm studying photographs and then slip them back into the larger envelope. There's no time to open the cards now, because my guests will be arriving soon. I hold the manila envelope to my chest, hugging this unexpected treasure, before I slide it under my pillow. The cards will wait for me there, twelve delicious secrets waiting to be revealed.

I sit on the front porch steps waiting for my guests. The mall is full of interesting sights. It's trick-or-treat day, which means kids get to walk around the mall in their Halloween costumes, collecting candy from participating stores. I have a bag of miniature candy bars on the porch, but so far nobody has come to our door. One little girl in a gauzy pink fairy costume got as far as the open gate, but then her mom ran up and yanked her back. Maybe parents don't want their kids crossing the train track.

A lot of the stores have Halloween decorations in their front windows. Black cats and jack-o'-lanterns and well-dressed mannequins sporting witches' hats. Discount Cell Phones has a ropy spider web inhabited by a fuzzy black spider the size of a dinner plate. I break out in goose bumps every time I glance at it.

Hal lumbers by, but I pretend not to see him. He looks tired and grumpy, probably because he had to work a double shift. The mall brings in extra security for special events like trick-or-treat day.

The security cameras have finally been repaired, and more have been added. My mother is still ranting about how it took four vandalism attacks to get Jack Caldwell moving on the issue. She's also ranting about the fact that there's now a camera pointing directly at our house. Every time I come out on the porch, I wave to it and stick my tongue out.

Robby is the first Mystery Grouper to arrive. He's wearing a black T-shirt with a skull and crossbones on the front, and a baseball cap decorated with orange jack-o'-lanterns.

"Look what I got at Zeke's Electronics," he says, holding out a candy bar as he plops down next to me. "I was walking by and this salesclerk stepped out of the store and handed it to me."

"You do look a little bit like a trick-or-treater," I tell him.

Robby holds up a DVD. "I got the movie. My dad had to take me to three different places before we found it." He slides the DVD across the porch, toward the front door. Then he breaks his candy bar into two pieces and hands me one of them. We sit on the porch steps coating our teeth in caramel-y chocolate as we watch all the little vampires and ghosts and witches ambling along. Every time the train goes by, we wave to the passengers.

"Hey," Robby says after a while. "You know how a lot of sports teams name themselves after scary wild animals, like the Bears, the Panthers, the Tigers? Wouldn't it be cool if they used Halloween monster names instead?"

I frown. "You mean like Frankenstein?"

"More like werewolves and stuff. I mean, if you want to sound tough, what could be better than a monster name? Think of it—the Denver Vampires, the Miami Werewolves, the New York Zombies. Scary, huh? Plus, the mascot costumes would be awesome."

"How about the New York Blobs?" I say. "Did you ever see that old movie *The Blob?* Now that's a scary monster."

"Oh. Here come the twins," Robby says, getting to his feet.

Kenny and Kevin wave as they come down the

walk, but instead of joining us on the porch, they veer into the yard and disappear around the side of the house.

"They want to investigate your house," Robby says. "They're working on the Shadow Vandal case."

"Ah," I say, the truth finally dawning. "That's why they wanted to have the party here."

Kenny and Kevin are very interested in my mystery. Every time our reading group meets, the first thing they do is ask about the latest developments. Kevin writes notes in a little notepad that reminds me of Officer Sanford's.

Ash is the last guest to arrive. She's wearing designer jeans and a softer-than-soft pale green sweater that I recognize as cashmere. You won't ever see me in cashmere because it's too expensive. But every August when the new cashmere sweaters arrive at Farringer's, I browse amongst them, petting them like they were kittens, pushing my face into their softness, sometimes even daring to try one on.

Ash greets Robby and me with a tight nod and shoves a bag of cheese curls at me. Robby leans over the porch bannister and calls for the twins, and we all troop into the house.

"Well, hello, everybody," says my mother, coming into the living room.

We go through introductions, and my mother chats briefly with each of my guests. Then she retreats to her bedroom to do some work on her computer, telling us to yell if we need anything. I'm glad she's not the kind of mom who hovers, and I'm pretty sure the others appreciate this, too.

"How about if we start with the snacks and then

watch the movie," Robby suggests, tearing open the bag of cheese curls.

"Sure," I say, grateful that he's taking the lead in moving things along. I've never hosted a social gathering before and am not sure how to go about it.

In addition to the cheese curls, we have potato chips, pretzels, French onion dip, store-bought chocolate chip cookies, a jug of iced tea, and a two-liter bottle of cola.

Robby and I sit at the kitchen table munching away while Ash stands at the window watching the train go by and Kevin and Kenny roam the house looking for clues. The twins have been dying to explore my house for so long, I know they won't stop until they've searched every square inch.

I hear them in the living room, fiddling with the bolt on the front door and opening and closing windows. "Ow!" says one of them. I figure he must have tried to look up the chimney and got hit by something on its way down.

The twins walk through the kitchen. They open the door to the cellar.

"There's nothing down there," I say sharply. "Hey, enough already, guys. We're here to watch a movie, not solve the mall mystery."

"No reason we can't do both," Kenny says, clomping down the steps with Kevin close behind.

There are scraping sounds, rustling noises. A distant, metallic bang, like somebody bumped into the washer. A brief discussion in low, murmuring voices.

"Guys! Come on," I call down the stairs. "You're missing the party."

They troop up the stairs, their footsteps trudging

and reluctant.

"Find anything interesting?" asks Robby.

"No," Kenny says, glowering at me, "because we didn't have enough time to do a good search."

"Hey, why don't we move the party to the cellar?" Kevin says. "We could set everything up in that room with the couch and—"

"No!" The word whooshes out of my mouth as forcefully as erupting lava. Everybody stares at me.

"I mean…" I force myself to smile. "It's not very nice down there. It's just an icky old cellar. Let's stay up here."

Ash steps away from the window. "I vote we go to the cellar. It would be more private."

I look at Robby, mentally begging him to disagree, but he's not even looking at me. He says, "Yeah, let's do it."

Everybody starts gathering up the party stuff. I have no choice but to follow as they head down the stairs. I keep telling myself I'll be fine since four other people will be down there with me. But the listening half of me isn't buying it.

"Hey, does this thing work?" asks Robby, fingering the knob on the ancient console stereo that belonged to my grandpa.

"Cool!" he says, when tinny, old-fashioned music erupts from the speakers. The radio is still set to the station my grandpa used to listen to. The stereo hasn't been turned on since before he died. I'm surprised it still works.

Robby turns the dial until he finds a station playing our kind of music. "That's better," he says, cranking up the volume.

I sink into the old brown couch, and a puff of musty air wafts around my face. I try to breathe away the lump of dread in my chest. Why do I always feel this way down here? Why am I afraid of my cellar?

Kenny and Kevin are prowling around like velociraptors, peering under furniture, peeling up the edges of the carpet, rapping on walls. Robby has gotten into the spirit of the search, too. He's going through drawers in the old nightstand that's parked next to the couch. Ash, holding a plastic cup of cola, is standing in the middle of the little room like she's afraid to touch anything for fear of getting dirty. She has to keep moving out of the boys' way.

My heart just about stops when Kenny steps up to the furnace room door and jiggles the doorknob. He turns to me. "What's in here?"

"Nothing," I say. "That's just the furnace room."

"I'd like to take a look. Where's the key?"

"I don't know. I think we lost it."

I keep my eyes down, because I know Kenny will see the lie busting out of them if I look at him.

"Chloe?" calls my mother from the top of the stairs.

"Yeah?" I call back.

She clunks halfway down the stairs. "I have to run down to the store." She has to shout to be heard over the music. "Vanessa just called. There's something going on."

"Like what?"

"I don't know. Maybe the cash register went offline again. I could hardly hear her—there was a lot of background noise. Then we got cut off, or she hung up. I'll be back in a few minutes, okay?"

With my mother gone, my feeling of dread intensifies. I take a pretzel from the bowl and put it back uneaten. I reach for the iced tea but then change my mind. My very soul feels itchy. Unable to contain myself a second longer, I jump up off the couch.

"Guys. Let's go upstairs and watch the movie."

Kenny and Kevin grunt and disappear into the laundry room. Robby and Ash totally ignore me. Robby is contemplating the junk stashed under the stairs—a banged-up bookcase, two lamps, a couple of cardboard boxes, the lawn chair. Ash is studying a painting of a farm that hangs on the wall behind the couch.

"Maybe I'll just go upstairs and start watching the movie without you," I say. "How about that?"

No response.

"Guys! Come on," I say.

"Soon," Robby says vaguely. He has opened one of the cardboard boxes under the stairs and is lifting out a stack of Grandma Lamont's dishes.

"You better not break any of those," I say irritably. "What are you looking for, anyway?"

"The spray paint can. The vandal could have stashed it anywhere. It'll have his fingerprints on it. If we find it, we can give it to the police. They can run a fingerprint check, and hopefully they'll be able to nab the guy."

"Are you crazy?" I sputter. "That can has my fingerprints on it, too. I'll end up being the one who gets arrested!"

"Guys!" says Kenny. He's standing at the furnace room door. I didn't even notice that he and Kevin had returned from the laundry room. "I think I found that missing key." To my dismay, he slides his hand behind the bureau next to the furnace room door and comes out with the key. He holds it up triumphantly, like a fisherman displaying a supersized trout, and then turns to the locked door.

"No!" I scream. "You can't go in there!"

Chapter 29

Finally I have everybody's attention. Nobody's more surprised than I am by my outburst. It's like a stranger stepped into my head and spoke through my mouth.

"Why don't you want us going in there?" asks Kenny, his gaze fixed on me.

"Because—because—" My heart is pounding, my mouth dry. "I don't know. I don't know why I said that."

"Why do you keep that door locked, anyway?" asks Kevin.

"Because—we just do. We always have."

The twins exchange a look that involves mirror-image cocked eyebrows.

"We have to go in there," Kenny says to me. "It's the only room we haven't searched."

"No, don't. Please!"

And suddenly I'm crying. I bury my face in my hands so nobody will see my blotchy, scrunched-up face. When I peek through my fingers, I see Ash staring at me, her eyes wide. I turn my back on her. Why does she, of all people, have to be here to witness this?

"Chloe," Kenny says, sounding like somebody's stern dad. "You better tell us what's going on."

"Okay!" I give a loud sniffle and wipe my snotty nose on the back of my hand. "I'm scared of my cellar.

There, are you happy? I always thought it was some little-kid thing I'd grow out of, but I never did. And now—now it seems like it's the furnace room that's behind it all, though I don't know why that would be."

"Gotta be a reason," says Robby, carefully lowering Grandma Lamont's dishes back into their cardboard box.

"And we're going to find out what it is," says Kenny. He inserts the key into the lock and opens the furnace room door.

"Kenny—no!" My voice breaks off on a fresh sob.

"Robby," says Ash in a hushed, urgent voice. "Go get Mrs. Lamont."

Robby takes the steps two at a time. The ceiling above us creaks as he races for the front door.

"We're just going to take a quick look around," Kenny says, giving me a reassuring salute, like a departing sea captain.

"Real quick," Kevin says.

"I really wish you wouldn't," I say, just to make sure my feelings on the subject are known.

"Come on, Chloe," says Ash, tugging at my sleeve. "Let's wait for your mom upstairs."

"Fine!" I wrench myself out of her grasp and stomp up the stairs.

In the living room, I plop down on the couch with a box of tissues. I blot my eyes and blow my nose hard.

Ash is sitting in the rocking chair in the corner, rocking slightly as she watches me.

I fling my used tissue on the floor and glare at her. "You're just loving this, aren't you? I bet you can't wait to tell everybody at school. 'Chloe's a big baby. Chloe's scared of her cellar—' "

"I'm not telling anybody anything," she says. "I'm not like that."

"Yeah, right," I say, rolling my eyes. "I think everybody knows what you're like."

"Oh my gosh." Abruptly she gets to her feet, leaving the rocking chair rocking violently behind her. "I'm so sick of this. Why do people think I'm a jerk just because my family has money?"

"People don't think you're a jerk because you have money. They think you're a jerk because you think you're better than everybody else."

"What?" She looks genuinely wounded. "I don't think I'm better than everybody else."

"Well, you sure come across that way. And I gotta tell you—trying to get my poem disqualified? Didn't help your image one bit."

She stamps her foot. "That wasn't me! That was my dad."

"Really?" I say, studying her through narrowed eyes. "You're sure it wasn't just a little bit you?"

"Are you kidding? I was, like, totally humiliated by the whole thing! I thought you deserved to win. Your poem is so good, much better than mine. I begged my dad not to go to the school board. So did my mom. But he wouldn't listen. He can't stand it when I don't win."

She's pacing around the tiny room now, agitated as a caged tiger.

"He makes me take all these lessons—tennis, ice skating, piano, French—and he expects me to be the best at all of them. That poem he brought to the school board meeting? I wrote it in fourth grade. I didn't write anything new for the contest because I didn't have time. Because of all those lessons! But he made me enter anyway."

She looks at me, and I'm startled by the despair brimming in her eyes. "My dad doesn't care about me. I'm just something he owns, like his car or his home theater or his big stupid boat. He wants to be able to brag about me, and when he can't, he gets mad. He calls me stupid, incompetent, clumsy. I hate him! I wish he'd leave me alone."

It takes me a minute to digest all this. I never would have pegged Ash as an oppressed individual, though when I think back on her dad's tantrum at the school board meeting, it makes sense.

I feel a sudden, overwhelming sadness for Ash, and an odd connection with her, too. It seems we both have big holes in our lives where a father should be. But as sad as my situation is, I think hers is a little bit sadder.

"So let me get this straight," I say. "You entered a fourth-grade poem in the seventh-grade poetry contest? And Dr. Pelesky said she would have given it sixth place? That's pretty good, actually."

She lets out a noise that's half sob, half laugh.

And then two things happen in rapid succession.

Kenny and Kevin come bounding out of the cellar like a pair of cheetah-chased gazelles.

"Chloe! Chloe, we found something!"

"You won't believe it—"

"—there's a secret passageway in your cellar!"

That stunning proclamation barely has time to travel from my ears to my brain before Robby comes bursting through the front door, all out of breath. "Guys! Something's going on. There's nobody in the mall—not a single person!"

Chapter 30

Without even discussing it, we decide the empty mall situation needs to be investigated first. We swarm out the front door and come to a halt on the porch, looking around in bewilderment.

The corridors are starkly empty, the stores unattended, though soothing instrumental music continues to play from the loudspeakers. None of the security gates are in place, which suggests people left in a hurry.

I feel a stab of abandonment. Where is my mother? Why didn't she come back to get me?

I squeeze my eyes shut, trying to will things back to normal. Wishing, praying. When I open them, the mall is still empty. It's like we've been snatched out of our comfortable, familiar lives and dropped into one of those movies where everyone on Earth disappears except for a small band of people who face assorted dangers as they try to survive.

"We need to get out of here," Ash says in a shaky voice.

"Hold on," says Robby. "We don't know what's going on. It could be anything—a nuclear attack, a tornado, an outer space invasion. Maybe we're better off staying in here."

Ash is wide-eyed. "Outer space invasion!"

"I doubt if that's it," I say, glaring at Robby.

"Shh!" Kevin holds up a hand. "Do you hear that?"

"Yes!" says Kenny. "It's voices. People talking."

Ash, Robby, and I don't hear anything but shopping music, yet the twins insist there are voices. They lead the way across the train track, around the picket fence, and down the corridor into Farringer's.

"There!" says Robby. "I hear it, too. People talking."

We all hear it now. We exchange nods of relief and hurry toward the murmuring voices, eager to find people who will tell us what's going on. Grownups who will take charge of the situation.

On the left side of the store, near the front, is the electronics department. The voices get louder as we approach. My heart sinks as I realize what it is we've been hearing.

Ash realizes, too. "Oh. It's not people talking. It's the TVs."

"That's okay," says Robby. "At least we can find out what's going on. If it's big enough to empty out a mall, it'll be big enough to be on the news."

He plants himself in front of a TV that's wider than I am tall and flicks through the channels until he finds a local station.

"There!" says Kevin, pointing to the screen.

The scene shows the Oasis Mall in the distance, its parking lot a concrete desert emptied of cars. In the foreground are several fire trucks and police cars, their lights flashing urgently. A disembodied male voice is speaking. "—was evacuated at approximately two forty-five this afternoon in response to the bomb threat. The Regional Bomb Task Force has been summoned and is expected to arrive shortly. Anyone living within a one-mile radius is being urged to evacuate…"

"Bomb threat!" Ash stares at the TV in disbelief. "Why didn't anybody tell us?"

"They probably tried," I say. "If a security guard knocked on the door, we never heard him because the music was turned up so loud." I glance pointedly at Robby, but he's still gazing at the TV, his posture so relaxed, he might be watching a sitcom from the safety of his own living room. "The guard probably figured we already got out."

Suddenly, all the TVs go dark. The lights go out, too. Somebody in our little group gasps dramatically, probably Ash. A few seconds later, the lights flick back on, but they're different. Dim, yellowish, like the lighting in a horror movie.

"Uh…what just happened?" asks Kevin.

"The power went out," I tell him. "The emergency generator kicked on. The generator has enough power to keep some lights on, but nothing else is going to work."

"Why'd the power go out?" Kenny asks me. "Does it have something to do with the bomb threat?"

"How would I know? I've never been through a bomb threat before."

"Okay. We really need to get out of here," Ash says, and this time nobody argues.

We thread our way through Farringer's, heading for the exit between Housewares and Luggage. Robby stops to admire a black leather jacket in the Young Men's department. I grab his arm and literally drag him away.

When we reach the exit, we find that all four doors are locked. Kenny keeps throwing his weight against one, like maybe it's just stuck, until I tell him to stop. When the doors are locked, they're locked from both the outside and the inside.

"What the heck?" Kenny says, glaring at me like this is my fault.

Everybody else is staring at me, too, so I explain. "The mall started out with the kind of locks you can open from the inside just by pushing on the door. But then a couple of years ago, these two guys hid in Farringer's at closing time. Their friends showed up with a van, and the two guys let them into the store. They stole a bunch of stuff—TVs, computers, cameras, jewelry."

"Jerks," mutters Kevin.

"Tell me about it. The security alarm went off as soon as they opened the door, but by the time the guard got down there, they were driving away." The guard, of course, was pokey old Hal. "The police never caught them. The same thing happened a couple of weeks later, and this time they got Hart's department store. Jack—that's the guy who owns the mall—he was like, 'This has to stop.' So he had the locks changed. Now the doors are on an automatic system that locks them from the outside and the inside."

A few seconds of silence tick past. Then Ash says, "Well, this is just great," sounding like the crisis is a missed bus, not imminent death. But she's as white as the fine china in Farringer's Housewares department. "Locked in the mall with a bomb that's about to go off."

"There's no bomb," Kenny says, scoffing. "I can almost guarantee it."

"Me too," says Robby. "We had a bomb threat

once at my school back in New Mexico. It turned out to be a false alarm. Just somebody playing a prank. The teachers took us outside while the police searched the building." He grins. "Anytime you get to have recess instead of math class, it's a good day."

"Well, I would not call this a good day," Ash says reprovingly.

"Guys, look," says Kevin. He's standing at a nearby checkout counter, pointing at a phone. "We can call nine-one-one."

"Actually, we can't," I say. "The phone system is hooked into the computer network, which runs on electricity. When the power's off, so are the computers and the phones."

Ash stamps her foot. "I hate this mall!"

"Calling for help, though—that's a good idea," Kenny says. "Anybody have a cell phone?"

"I do," Ash says sourly. "It's back home on my dresser. My mom wouldn't let me bring it because she was afraid I'd spend the afternoon texting my friends instead of working on our project."

"Aw. You wouldn't do that, would you?" says Robby.

Ash considers that. "Yeah, I probably would."

"I use my mom's phone sometimes," I say. "But she has it with her today."

"I'm getting one for my thirteenth birthday, in February," Robby says with a grin. "But I guess that doesn't help us now."

"Yeah, we don't have one either," says Kevin. "Our parents think they're too expensive."

"We've been nagging them about it," adds Kenny. "They finally got us walkie-talkies to shut us up."

"Like that's the same," Kevin says petulantly.

We glance around at each other, waiting for somebody to come up with a new idea. Finally Kenny says, "We might not be locked in. Sure, mall security probably locked most of the doors to make sure some idiot doesn't sneak back inside. But they probably left at least one door unlocked so the bomb squad can get in."

"Is that possible, Chloe?" Kevin asks. "Can the mall people unlock just one door? Or a couple?"

I nod. "They do that during the holiday shopping season when one or two of the stores are open really early and the others aren't."

"Great!" says Kenny. He and Kevin exchange triumphant nods. "So, which door do you think might be unlocked?"

I think that over. "Probably the one my mom and I use, by the mall office. Actually, that door isn't on the automatic locking system. You have to use a key."

Ash's face lights up. "Ooh! Do you have a key?"

"No. I mean, *we* have a key, Mom and me, but she keeps it on her keychain. Which is in her purse, which is with her right now, wherever she might be."

Ash stamps her foot again. Robby says, "We should check that door anyway. Maybe they forgot to lock it."

We troop into the corridor. At least it's brighter out here, thanks to the skylights. I lead the way to the exit by the mall office. Nobody seems surprised when we find the door locked.

Kevin says if we can get into the mall office, maybe we can figure out how to unlock the automatic doors. I'm not sure if the automatic system works when the electricity is off, though I don't say anything about that. I'm sick of being the person who keeps shooting down everybody's ideas. In the end it doesn't matter, because the mall office door is locked, too.

We mill around like lost ants, not sure what to do next. I study my fellow Mystery Groupers, noting their differing reactions. Kenny and Kevin are half-grinning like they're having the time of their lives. Robby, shoving a quarter into a bubblegum machine, seems unconcerned. Ash looks anxious, yet peeved, as though her involvement in this misadventure is a mistake the universe had better sort out quickly—or else. As for me, I'm worried, but all in all I feel much better than I felt in my cellar.

"So," says Robby, the word slurred by the huge pink sphere of bubble gum he just popped into his mouth. "I guess we just wait for the bomb guys to show up and get us out."

"Or," I say, "we keep looking for an unlocked door. Because we don't know how long it's going to take for the bomb guys to get here, and maybe—just maybe—there really is a bomb. I don't know about you guys, but if there is, I don't want to be around when it goes off."

Robby makes a be-my-guest gesture with his hand. "Lead the way, Mall Girl."

I shoot him a murderous look and set off for the main corridor.

"So, Kenny, Kevin," says Ash. "Tell us about the secret passageway you found in Chloe's cellar."

"What?" exclaims Robby. "You found an actual secret passageway?"

I make a huffy noise and walk faster, trying to put

some distance between me and the conversation. Why do they have to talk about this now?

"Yeah, there's this wall with shelves on it in the furnace room," Kenny says. "It's actually a hidden door. I pulled on a shelf, and the door opened right up."

"How did you know to do that?" asks Ash.

"Kev figured it out. He noticed cool air coming out of a crack around the shelves. You wouldn't have that if there was a solid wall behind them."

"Where does the passageway go?" Robby asks.

"Don't know," Kevin replies. "As soon as we found it, we ran upstairs to tell the girls. Hey, Chloe," he calls. "Where do you think the passageway goes? Do you think your mom knows about it?"

"Don't ask *me*," I say icily. "I didn't even know it was there."

"Maybe it leads to a secret room with a dead body inside," Robby says gleefully. "Or a prison cell with medieval torture devices. Or a portal to another dimension. Or the lair of some horrible underground monster!"

"Robby!" Ash says in exasperation.

"It probably just leads to the mall basement," says Kevin.

"Except it doesn't," I shoot back, "because the mall doesn't have a basement."

We lapse into silence. For a while there's only the sound of scuffing feet and an occasional snapping noise from Robby as he pops a bubble. Those bubble-gum noises are surprisingly loud and echo-y in the empty mall, like muted pink gunshots.

We pass the pet store. The familiar smells of dry dog food, tropical fish tanks, and parakeet poop waft up my nose. I resist the urge to run in and check on the kittens.

It's Kevin who finally breaks the silence. "You realize what this means."

"What *what* means?" asks Ash.

"The secret passageway. It's how the Shadow Vandal has been getting into Chloe's house. And into the mall."

Chapter 31

Like a choreographed quintet, we come to a halt, instantly reassembling into a loose football huddle. Everybody but me is talking, and there's so much overlapping chatter, I don't know who's saying what.

"It explains everything!"

"—the missing eggs, the spray paint—"

"The knife on the floor!"

"—how the doors were always bolted from the inside—"

"—how the security guard saw the Shadow Vandal run down the Farringer's wing and disappear—"

"It was because he ran into Chloe's house—"

"—and escaped through the secret passageway!"

"Guys!" I yell. Everybody shuts up. "We don't know any of this for sure. Just because there's a secret passageway in my cellar doesn't mean the Shadow Vandal's been using it."

"True," Robby says. "But it sure explains a lot."

"I can't wait to explore that passageway!" Kevin says. "The second this bomb business is over, we're going down there with flashlights."

"We so are," Robby agrees joyfully.

"Oh no, you're not," I retort. "There are probably spiders down there. Humongous ones, as big as your hand."

Spiders? Where did that come from?

Robby lets out a surprised laugh. "You think humongous spiders live under the mall?"

I'm in the cave again, in the middle of a passageway...

Except maybe it's not a cave. Maybe it's the secret passageway in my cellar.

"Oh!" I clamp a hand over my mouth.

"What?" says Ash.

Haltingly, I tell the Mystery Groupers about the spider dream.

"Wow," says Ash. "So you think this dream of yours isn't just a dream? That it's something that really happened to you—in the secret passageway?"

"No." I shake my head in a way that's more denial than certainty. "I've never been in that secret passageway. I didn't even know it existed till Kenny and Kevin found it."

"So...what, then?" Ash frowns. "You think the dream was a premonition? Like, a warning of what's to come?"

"No!" The idea that I will be attacked by freakishly large spiders in the future is even more horrifying than the idea that I was attacked in the past.

"So if it's not a memory and it's not a premonition," says Kenny, "that leaves a random dream. And if that's all it is, there's nothing to be afraid of."

"Are you sure you've never been in there?" Robby persists.

"I'm sure, Roberto." My words come out like angry bullets. "If I was in there before, I think I'd remember it."

"Not necessarily," says Ash. "What if something

happened in there a long time ago? Something so scary that you repressed the memory?"

"Oh, so now you're a licensed psychologist," I say.

"No, but I used to go to one. I know some things."

I try to keep my face neutral as I process this interesting new fact about Ash.

"Whatever happened to you in that passageway," Ash goes on, "it's been haunting your subconscious. That's why you keep having the dream. That's why you're so scared of your cellar."

Robby is nodding excitedly. "We should hypnotize her, take her back to whatever happened in there." He looks around. "Does anybody know how to do hypnosis?"

"Nobody's going to hypnotize me," I snap.

Kevin makes an awkward throat-clearing noise. "You know, I'm thinking maybe the spiders-as-big-as-your-hand part didn't actually happen. That's something out of an old Indiana Jones movie."

"Believe what you want," I say. "But if you go in there—and I'm not saying I'll let you—definitely take bug spray with you."

We move on. Novelty Gifts for Less has been playing Halloweenish music all day, and as we get closer, we hear the upbeat strains of "Ghostbusters." The song blasts our eardrums as we pass the store and then fades as we move farther away. Finally the loudspeaker music claims the air again. An instrumental song is playing, a tense, moody piece that makes a fitting soundtrack for our situation but doesn't help my frame of mind one bit. I'd rather have "Ghostbusters," which at least *sounds* cheerful, even if it's about ghosts.

As we near Deluca's Sporting Goods, the others

are still yapping about the secret passageway. I tune them out. I glance wistfully into Connie's Cupboard, half-expecting to see my mother waving from behind the counter. I've never seen the store deserted before, the beautiful wares unattended. A wave of childlike longing engulfs me—*I want my mommy!* I force the feeling away and head into Deluca's.

We try the exit doors at the rear of the store. They're all locked.

"This is getting old," Ash says as we head back into the corridor. "How many more exits do we have to check?"

"A lot," I tell her. "We haven't even hit the upper level yet."

Kenny nudges me. "Hey. Chloe." He's giving me a crafty, heavy-lidded look, the kind a used-car salesman might adopt just before offering a customer a square deal. "Do you really want to get out of here?"

I stare back sardonically. "Uh, yeah, Kenny, I really do."

"Then let's go back to your house."

"Why?"

"The secret passageway," says Kevin, moving in like a basketball player stealing the ball. "It's obviously a way out."

"What? You don't know that," I say. "Besides, there's probably something bad in there, like Robby said."

"Hey, don't listen to me," says Robby. "I was just throwing out ideas." He edges closer to the twins, making it clear whose side he's on. "This might be our only chance to explore the passageway. Once Chloe's mom finds out about it, she'll tell the police, and they'll probably block it off so nobody can get in. I say we check it out now."

"No!" Ash and I shout at the same moment.

I shoot Ash a grateful look, glad she's with me on this.

But the twins are determined, and with Robby on their team, Ash and I are quickly overruled. The guys decide that two of them will go through the secret passageway while the third continues to investigate mall exits with Ash and me. Whoever gets out first will send help for the others.

The question is, which two guys will explore the secret passageway? All three are itching to go.

"Flip a coin," Ash suggests.

"There are three of us," says Robby. "A coin only has two sides."

"Flip three coins," I say. "The winners will be the two who get the same side."

Robby fishes a penny and two dimes out of his jeans pocket and doles out the dimes to Kenny and Kevin.

"Ready…set…go," says Ash. The boys toss their coins into the air, catch them, and slap them down on the backs of their hands.

All three coins show tails.

"Again," commands Ash.

Toss, catch, slap. This time Kenny and Robby get heads, while Kevin ends up with tails.

Robby leaps upward, whooping with joy as he punches the air. "Yes!"

"Best two out of three?" Kevin says, his face oddly pale.

Robby laughs. "Nice try, Kev."

He starts to walk away. Kenny grabs his arm.

"Robby. Are you sure you don't want to stay with the girls? I mean, seeing how you and Chloe are such good friends and all."

"I'm sure," says Robby. "No offense, Mall Girl."

I study Kenny and Kevin. They're standing close together, their expressions so stricken, you'd think they just swallowed poison. I suddenly realize the problem—they're not used to being apart. Like, ever.

But because I'm tired and cranky and on edge, I just can't dredge up any sympathy.

"The coin flip was fair and square," I say. "Robby and Kenny, get out of here. You'll find flashlights in the kitchen, in the drawer at the bottom of the stove. Kevin, come on. You're with Ash and me."

And so the twins are wrenched apart for the first time in maybe forever. Kenny keeps turning around and walking backwards, throwing anguished glances our way. Kevin stands perfectly still as he watches his brother go, his fists clenched at his side.

"Let's get going," I say brusquely, turning away so I won't have to look at Kevin's face.

I lead the way to the exit at the end of the Deluca's corridor. I'm not surprised to find all four doors locked. My sunbathing site is just beyond the glass, so close I can almost smell the mulch. But it might as well be on the moon, because we can't get there.

We tromp back toward the main corridor. I keep throwing glances at Kevin. He hasn't said a word since Kenny left. I thought I'd feel safer having one of the guys with Ash and me, but I was wrong. Kevin is dead weight. His feet are dragging, his head bowed. He's like somebody in mourning.

Ash and I continue to discuss our situation, theorizing about which upper-level exits are most likely to be open. Kevin doesn't even chime in.

"Oh, for crying out loud," I finally say. That's what my mother says when she's totally exasperated. "Kevin, just go already. Go back to my house. If you run really fast, you can probably catch up with Kenny and Robby."

Kevin raises his head, and in that instant I see life flooding back into his face. "You—you want me to go? Really?"

"Really," I say. "Ash and I are perfectly capable of checking exits on our own. It won't be for much longer, anyway. The bomb guys should be here any minute."

Kevin beams me a look of pure joy and takes off at a sprint down the corridor, the slap of his sneakers echoing through the empty air.

I wait for Ash to tear into me, but all she says is, "The twins are really lost without each other, aren't they?"

"Yes," I say. "They are."

The Faidley family, I've learned, is a large one, and Kenny and Kevin are sandwiched between older and younger siblings.

Maybe their parents were already frazzled by too many kids when the twins came along, two babies for the price of one. It was probably easier for them to treat Kenny and Kevin like a single child instead of separate individuals, and maybe they never stopped doing that. It would explain why the twins act like two halves of a whole.

But in my opinion they need to conquer this separation anxiety before they get much older.

As Ash and I turn down the main corridor, we hear the sound of glass breaking from above.

"What now?" I say with a sigh.

Chapter 32

We head for the nearest escalator, halfway down the main corridor. We have to walk up, because the power is still off. When we finally get upstairs, it's Ash who spots something amiss. "Over there, at Royal Jewelers. Somebody smashed the front window."

Our shoes crunch across the broken glass. Not only has the window been smashed, but the jewelry that was on display is missing. All the really expensive stuff that's kept locked up, including the necklace Robby photographed for the contest.

"Looters," Ash says, and when I look at her questioningly, she explains. "People who steal stuff during disasters. My uncle owns some stores in Kansas, and he says a lot of looting goes on after tornadoes. Stores are closed with their windows blown out from the wind, and people go inside and just start taking stuff."

Her eyes rove over the jagged frame of glass rimming the display window. "I'm guessing when the bomb threat got announced today, somebody saw their big chance. They probably hid while the mall was being evacuated and then came out and started stealing stuff. Nobody was here to stop them."

I glance around nervously. "So somebody else is trapped in the mall with us. A not very nice somebody."

"I kind of wish we'd stuck with the guys," Ash

admits.

“We might still be able to catch up with them.”

She looks at me in surprise. “But you’re scared of the secret passageway.”

“You know what I’m more scared of? Running into some looter who doesn’t want any witnesses. Come on. Let’s go back to the house.”

We slink along the wall like cat burglars, duck low as we creep down the escalator. When we reach the Farringer’s wing, we race for my house. But as I’m crossing the railroad track, my foot gets caught. Down I go, twisting my ankle in a direction it was never meant to turn.

“Ow!” I’m on the ground, rocking in pain. “I think I just broke my ankle.”

“Oh, Chloe.” Ash pulls me up. “Here, lean on me.”

We hobble up the porch steps and stumble through the door into the dim house. Ash deposits me on the couch and locks and bolts the front door. Then she fumbles with the lamp on the end table.

“The lights aren’t going to work,” I tell her. “Our house isn’t on the generator system.”

She reaches behind the couch and yanks the drapes apart, letting in more light from the skylighted corridor. Gently, she folds up the right leg of my jeans. My ankle is all puffed up and getting purpler by the second.

“I think it’s just sprained,” says Ash. “I had a sprained ankle once, and it looked like that. Come on, I’ll help you to the cellar.”

“Uh…” Now that I’m in the house, I’m quickly losing my nerve. “Maybe you should go without me. I’d just slow you down. I can wait here.”

She shakes her head. “You wouldn’t be safe.”

"Sure I would. The door's bolted."

"Do you really think a bolt's going to keep a looter out? If he decides to loot your house, he'll smash a window. And with that ankle, you won't be able to run away."

I sigh wretchedly. "Fine. I'll come."

Ash fetches flashlights from the kitchen. She helps me down the cellar steps and into the furnace room. There's a small bench just inside. Ash eases me onto it.

"You okay?" she asks.

I shake my head somberly. My heart is drumming a frenzied beat, and there's a scream gathering at the back of my throat.

"Just sit there for a minute," Ash says. "Relax. Look around. This is a nice room. A little dirty, but nice."

I draw in a deep, tremulous breath and shine my flashlight around. The furnace room is smallish, about the size of my bedroom. The old rusty-dusty furnace, which we no longer use, and the water heater, which we do use, are in a rectangular nook to the right. Grandpa's carpentry area is to the left. I survey the long table, still flecked with sawdust, and the empty shelves that once held an assortment of tools. The scent of raw wood still lingers, a ghost of the boards Grandpa Glen once sawed and sanded.

A flash of memory pops into my head, as pink and friendly as Robby's bubblegum. I'm in this very room with a kindly old man who is grinning down at me. Grandpa Glen. My whole being feels like a giant smiley face because my grandpa has just given me a glossy brown wooden rocking horse he made himself. I'm rocking exuberantly on my new stallion, a miniature cowgirl giggling in delight.

That memory was lost to me until now because I would never let myself think about the furnace room. I suddenly see how crazy that was. The furnace room is a good place.

"You're smiling," says Ash. "Feeling better?"

"A little."

"Great. So how do we open this secret door?" She reaches toward the shelves and then pulls her hand back. "Ew. That old wood could give a person splinters."

Reluctantly, I limp over to her. Like Kevin, I can feel cool air flowing from a vertical crack at the edge of the shelving unit. When I look closely, I see it's more than a crack. It's the outline of a door.

I grasp the rough wood of one of the shelves and give a mighty tug. A door-sized section of wall swings outward.

Ash clucks in amazement. A rectangle of darkness lies before us. I hold my breath as Ash steps inside.

"Kenny? Kevin? Robby?"

No response.

"They must have gotten out." She shines her flashlight into the passageway and gives a little start. "Oh my gosh. Will you look at that."

I gasp. "What is it? Giant spiders? I knew it!"

She shoots me an exasperated glance. "Of course not." She takes a few steps into the passageway and comes back holding the missing spray paint can. "Looks like Kevin was right. The vandal's been using the secret passageway to get in and out of the mall."

I knew the vandal had to be coming through my house, but seeing hard evidence of it sends a shudder through me.

Ash motions me forward. "Check it out. It's pretty cool."

Apprehensively, I move forward and shine my flashlight into the secret passageway. The floor is a combination of packed dirt and bumpy rock. The walls are made of concrete block, and the ceiling is unfinished wooden planks shored up by pillars every few yards. The passage is slightly narrower than a hallway in somebody's house. It goes straight for maybe twenty-five feet and then disappears around a bend. I shine my light up and down, left and right. Not a spider is in sight.

"Obviously Robby and the twins got out," says Ash. "That means we can, too. Are you ready? We need to tell the police about the looter."

I open my mouth to say, "Sure, let's go," but what comes out instead is a hysterical little hiccup.

"I'm sorry," I tell Ash. "I can't stop thinking about spiders."

"Spiders," she repeats with a sigh. "Chloe, I really don't think—"

"I know you don't. But I do. I'm sorry, but I'm not going in there without bug spray."

"Okay. Where do you keep your bug spray?"

I shake my head mournfully. "We don't have any."

Living here, in the middle of the mall, Mom and I don't need it. We've never had a problem with creepy-crawlies.

"Deluca's probably sells it," says Ash. "I'll run down and grab a can."

"That's so far away! What if you run into the looter?"

"I won't. I know how to be careful."

I bow my head gratefully. "Thanks, Ash. I know it seems silly, but…"

"It's okay. If bug spray is what it takes to get you into that passageway, I will get you bug spray."

I push the shelf-door shut and trail Ash out to the family room to wait for her on the couch. My ankle still hurts, but not as badly as before. I can even put weight on it.

"Are you going to be okay down here all by yourself?" Ash asks.

"I think so. I'm actually feeling better about the cellar. Just hurry, okay?"

"I will."

I settle back against the couch, my mind whirling. As upsetting as this day has been, I'm hugely relieved to know that we've pretty much solved the Oasis Mall Mystery. Thanks to Kenny and Kevin, the police will now have a way to catch the Shadow Vandal. They can set a trap in the secret passageway and nab him the next time he shows up.

My mother and I will be off the hook. More important, the tension between us will be gone. We can get back to living our normal, boring mall lives.

Boom chucka chucka—I nearly jump out of my skin when music erupts from the stereo. At the same moment, the lamp next to the couch flicks on. Evidently the power has been restored—possibly by the bomb squad. It's good to have the lights working again, though I know it'll be a while before the mall's computer network and security cameras are back online.

I click off my flashlight and lean over the side of

the couch to turn off the stereo. The homey glow from the lamplight lends an air of cheer to the shabby room.

The front door opens. The ceiling creaks as feet move toward the cellar door.

I watch Ash start down the cellar stairs. I'm about to say, "That was fast," when an inner alarm jangles my every nerve.

The person on the stairs is not Ash. The posture is all wrong, the movements too graceless, and the build is that of a grown man, not a twelve-year-old girl. My horror increases when I notice that the person on the stairs is wearing a black sweatshirt with the hood up and is carrying a bulging pillowcase. It's one of our pillowcases. I recognize the blue and white striped pattern.

Oh. My. Gosh. The person coming down the stairs is the Shadow Vandal. And the mall looter. And undoubtedly, I think, the idea exploding in my brain as sure as dynamite, the person who called in the bomb threat.

Today's events are merely the vandal's latest attack on the mall. He wanted to empty it out so he could roam about freely, stealing whatever he wanted. And he probably shut off the electricity to disable the stores' security systems. If he hadn't, the police would have been notified the second he broke the display case at Royal Jewelers.

Knowing what I know, I should be trying to hide. But I'm paralyzed by terror, rooted in place like a spider immobilized by bug spray. The Shadow Vandal hasn't spotted me yet, but he soon will, because I'm sitting on the couch in lamp-lit glory, like a performer in the spotlight. He's hurrying down the stairs, the contents of the pillowcase clanking and rattling and tinkling with every step.

He reaches the bottom and turns right, into the cellar.

“Chloe!” He recoils so violently that his hood slips back, exposing his face.

I gasp. “You? You’re the Shadow Vandal?”

Chapter 33

"Kiddo," Ron Caldwell says in a faint, shocked voice. His mouth twists like he's trying to smile but can't remember how.

I'm dazed, incredulous—and, oddly, relieved. The Shadow Vandal isn't some sinister stranger. It's familiar old Uncle Ron. Uncle Ron, who I can talk to about anything.

"Wh-what are you doing here?" Ron asks, his voice unnaturally high, almost like a woman's. "They evacuated the mall—don't you know that?"

"I do know. But let's talk about you. What are you doing here? Oh, wait, I already know. You're making your getaway through the secret passageway. The same one you've been using all these months—to vandalize the mall!"

He swallows hard. "I know I have a lot to explain."

Tears of rage fill my eyes. "How could you, Uncle Ron? All these months, letting the police think I might be the vandal!"

He takes a step closer. "Now, they never actually accused you of anything. I made sure that didn't happen. They never had a shred of evidence."

"Even my mother wondered about me. My own mother! How could you do this to me, to us? And to your cousin? This is his mall."

"Chloe, please." He puts down his bag of loot.

"Can I just explain?"

"Yes. Explain." I lean forward, unblinkingly attentive.

Ron runs a hand up over his forehead, through his thinning hair. "Wow. Where to even... Well, for starters, I'm in love with your mother. Did you know that?" He lets out a brittle laugh as he sees my stunned expression. "I'm guessing you didn't."

"You're in love with my mother?" I repeat. "But that's crazy. You guys have never been...like that."

"No," he says wistfully. "Not yet. But we will be."

He sighs. "I fell in love with her in the tenth grade. Unfortunately, she was already your dad's girl. When he died, I stepped in to help her. I took care of you like you were my own child. I ran errands for her, I let her cry on my shoulder. I acted like a husband. But when I told her, Chloe, when I told her how I felt, you know what she said? She said she didn't feel the same way about me. She said we would never be anything but friends."

"Well then, that's that," I say. "If my mother doesn't love you, there's nothing you can do about it."

The lamplight is jaundicing his face, giving him a sickly look. I'm guessing I look the same way.

"She just needs time to get over your dad," he says. "The loss hit her hard. But she'll come around. She'll see I'm the man she was meant to be with. Her true love."

Indignation flares in me, quick as a flash fire. "My dad was her true love."

"She'll come around," Ron repeats, ignoring me, reassuring himself. "In time."

"Hey!" I say. "Can we get back to the vandalism

thing?"

His eyelids flutter, and he refocuses on me. "Yeah. Sure." He clears his throat. "A couple of months ago, out of the blue, I thought of the tunnel."

"The tunnel?" It takes me a second to realize he's talking about the secret passageway.

"It was supposed to have been filled in once the mall was complete. I started wondering if anyone had remembered to do that. So I checked. I opened up the creaky old trap door hidden outside the building and looked inside. And guess what? Nobody ever filled the tunnel in."

His gaze on me is almost tender. "You were so little the last time you were in there. Do you even remember it? After the spider incident, I didn't think you'd ever go in there again."

My heart lurches violently. "The spider incident?"

"It was just a tiny thing," he says with a thin, apologetic smile. "It didn't even bite you. But the way you carried on, I thought a man-eating tiger was down there with you."

"Oh!" I gasp as the memory hits me with the force of a breaking dam. Meanwhile, Ron is continuing to tell the story. His words mix with my own returning memory, creating a kind of stereo recollection that's almost too vivid to bear. It's like I'm three again, reliving the whole thing.

Ron was babysitting me one evening while my mother was out. We'd gone grocery shopping and had just gotten back. The passageway, or "tunnel," had been dug as a way for us to get safely in and out of our house while the construction was going on around us.

"I carried you down the steps," Ron says softly. "I

had to go back to the car to get the groceries. I gave you the flashlight and told you to stay put like a good little girl. While I was gone, a spider crawled over your hand. You dropped the flashlight, and it went out. By the time I got back, you were screaming bloody murder."

"Oh!" I say again, but this time it's because I'm remembering the other part of the story, the part Ron doesn't mention. The blackmail part.

At the time, my underdeveloped three-year-old brain thought he was trying to warn me, to protect me. After all, it was familiar old Uncle Ron talking, and he was doing it in a soothing Mr. Rogers voice. The threat existed only in his words.

"Now, you're not going to go telling your mother about this, are you, Chloe? How you were down here in the tunnel by yourself and got scared over some spider? Because if you told, that mean old spider might get angry and come after you. And this time it might bring a bunch of its friends."

Ron didn't want my mother to know he'd left me alone in the tunnel. My mother never left me alone anywhere, and if she'd known what he'd done, she'd have been furious. Not that it mattered, because in the end he never really stood a chance with her. But he didn't know that then. And he doesn't seem to know it now.

I use the back of my hand to swipe at my wet cheeks. Now at least I know the origin of my cellar phobia. And of the spider dream.

"Anyway," Ron goes on, "once I discovered the tunnel was still open, I started using it to get into your house. I'd go upstairs late at night and watch your mother sleep."

I can't help shuddering at the creepiness of that. I wonder if he watched me sleep, too. But I don't ask. I don't want him to get sidetracked again.

"One day when I was on my way to see Jack at the mall, I stopped to talk to one of the guards. He was griping about the security cameras not working and how Jack didn't seem to be in any hurry to fix them. I wasn't surprised. Jack was busy with the new mall in Clifton by then. Anytime my cousin has a new project in the works, he loses interest in the old ones. He's that way with women, too. No wonder he's on his third wife."

He shakes his head in mild contempt, and maybe envy, too. Ron, after all, hasn't had even one wife. "That was when I got the idea. I could use your house to get into the mall after hours and then do whatever I wanted. I could vandalize stores. With the security cameras down, nobody would ever know it was me."

He ends on a happily-ever-after note, like his story is finished. But he really hasn't told me much at all.

"But why did you decide to attack the mall in the first place?" I ask. "And why did you use our eggs, our spray paint? Why did you leave the knife on the kitchen floor where we'd find it?"

He runs his hand through his hair again, and I think maybe I've gotten all I'm going to get out of him. But then he looks me dead in the eye and says in a low, savage voice, "Because I wanted to make life hard for you. Because I wanted to drive your mother out of the mall. I wanted her to move her home and her business and her daughter and her life downtown with me, where she belongs.

"Now, granted"—abruptly his tone changes, and he's back to sounding like good-hearted Uncle Ron—"that wasn't my primary motive for the attacks. But I saw how it might be a very beneficial consequence. A way to kill two birds with one stone. I need her close to me, Chloe. I want us to be able to spend time together every single day, to nurture our love. Absence doesn't make the heart grow fonder. Togetherness does."

"For crying out loud, she doesn't love you!" I shout, wondering how he can be so blind to the truth. "She never has, she never will. And once she finds out about this—" I break off, knowing immediately that I've said the worst possible thing. Because this time it's going to take more than a spider to scare me into silence.

Ron cocks his head in surprise and mild reproach. "But how will she find out? You're not going to tell, are you? Would you really do that to your Uncle Ron? Your Uncle Ron who loves you both so much?"

I open my mouth and then close it again, dumbstruck by uncertainty. I want to say, "Of course not, Uncle Ron," but that would be a lie, and I'm not very good at lying.

I look away as I try to formulate a response, and when I look back, I see that Ron's gaze has wandered elsewhere. To the old fireplace poker propped in the corner by the steps. We haven't used that poker since the last time we had a fire to poke, a good nine years ago. Made of heavy iron, pointy at the poking end, it looks more like a weapon than a fireplace tool. And from the way Ron is looking at it, I know that's what he's thinking, too.

His eyes linger on the poker for only a few

seconds, but it's long enough. When he turns back to me, he can't help but see the terror in my eyes. Instantly his own eyes widen in anguish, remorse, and self-loathing.

"Oh, Chloe. No, no, no!" he says in a strangled voice. "Darling girl, I would never, never, not in a million years—"

But it's too late for that. Ron Caldwell considered, however briefly, doing something unspeakable to keep me from talking. And that's a horror we'll both have to live with for the rest of our lives.

A clatter from above startles us, and suddenly Ash is charging down the stairs screaming, "Get away from her, you jerk!" and she sprays Ron squarely in the face with bug spray.

He yowls in pain and drops to his knees, clawing at his eyes. Ash jumps from the fourth step to the floor like some cashmere-clad superhero and bounds over to me. "Chloe! Are you okay?"

I nod shakily.

"Let's get out of here," she says. Ron is between us and the stairs, so Ash yanks me into the furnace room. She tugs open the shelf-door without a word about splinters, and we move into the secret passageway, the place that has haunted my dreams for nearly a decade. And I'm fine. Like magic, the secret passageway has been rendered harmless, stripped of its spell over me.

My injured ankle lends an odd stitch to my gait—step-hitch, step-hitch—but I manage to keep up with Ash. She looks over every few seconds to make sure I'm okay.

When we round the bend, we catch a flurry of movement up ahead. It turns out to be two police officers—including Good Cop, who still could go to veterinary school if he really wanted to—followed by my mother, Robby, and the twins.

I choke out my tale about Ron, and the two policemen run toward the cellar while my mother and the boys usher Ash and me up a crude wooden staircase into the dazzlingly bright day-world. We're in a wooded nook, a miniature forest nestled between Farringer's and Sunglasses Galore. The trapdoor location is concealed behind overgrown shrubbery.

"Chloe!" sobs my mother, and suddenly we're in each other's arms, letting three months of pent-up liquid emotion flow out of us.

Chapter 34

Mom can't believe the tunnel is still open after all these years, though she admits the tunnel crossed her mind when our eggs first went missing. She checked the furnace room door that very day, and at various times afterward. She always found it locked, with no sign of tampering, which told her there had to be a different explanation. We were the only ones who had a key, or so she thought. She had forgotten about the key she'd given Ron all those years ago.

The rest of the day goes by in a blur. Ash and I and Robby and the twins give statements to the police. The bomb guys sweep the mall with their bomb-sniffing dogs and declare the whole building explosive-free. Not that they needed to bother with that. There was never any bomb. Ron confesses that to the police along with a whole bunch of other stuff.

Ron's main motive for vandalizing the mall, the motive he never got around to sharing with me because he was so busy mooning over my mother, was to ruin his cousin Jack. The cousins had been sports rivals in high school and business rivals since their early twenties. For a while, they'd lived in relative harmony, Ron building his downtown real estate empire, Jack helping his father oversee various projects in outlying areas.

But once the Oasis Mall was built, the power

shifted to Jack and his father. Stores and restaurants started leaving the downtown area. Everybody wanted to be in the glamorous new shopping mall on the outskirts of town. Pretty soon Ron owned more vacant buildings than occupied ones. Downtown was dying, its lifeblood sucked away by the bustling mall.

Ron, in his bitterness and desperation, cooked up a scheme to discredit the mall, to drive tenants back downtown. As he told me, he wanted my mother to be one of those tenants. And so, he decided to mess with her mind by using items from our house in his vandalism attacks. How he could do something so terrible to people he claimed to love is something I'll never understand.

As if emptying an entire mall on trick-or-treat day wasn't bad enough, Ron decided to steal some of the mall's more valuable merchandise—jewelry, electronics, and collectible items. He owed the county thousands of dollars in back taxes, and selling the stolen items would have let him pay a good portion of that debt.

I feel jarred after hearing these details, like I've fallen from a great height. Ron always seemed so nice. I wonder if maybe I'm not a good judge of character. Mom says I shouldn't beat myself up. He had her fooled, too.

****

It's nearly nine p.m. before Mom and I get home. I take a long, hot bath, and Mom makes me a cup of herbal tea, which I take to my room. I haven't forgotten about the twelve treasures waiting under my pillow. Although I'm not mad at my mother in any way, I close my door. This is between me and my grandparents.

With delicious anticipation, I slit open the first envelope. Inside is a card with a big pink bunny on the front. I open it, catching the twenty-dollar bill that falls out, and read the message inside.

Happy first birthday, Chloe! What a big girl you're getting to be. We LOVE, LOVE, LOVE you! Wish we could see you. Hugs and Kisses, Grandma and Grandpa Trimpey.

The handwritten messages get longer with each passing year. I get a raise every few years, too.

The card they sent when I turned ten blows me away. Along with thirty dollars, there's a photo of my parents when they were very young, maybe sixteen. They're all dressed up for a dance—not the prom, but some lesser high school bash, maybe a Valentine's Day dance, judging from my mother's pale pink dress. They're standing close together, hands locked, smiles radiant.

I can't stop staring at my father's hair. It's longish—and curly as can be. In all the pictures we have in our house, his hair is short. I mean, military-short, a few millimeters shy of shaved. He must have lopped off all those dysfunctional bedsprings when he hit adulthood, maybe in an attempt to look less boyish. But as a teenager, he was every bit as curly-headed as me.

This is what my grandma wrote inside the card.

Your father was a good man, Chloe. The best. We were so fond of him, and we were honored to have him as our son-in-law. Please understand, it wasn't that we didn't want him and your mother getting married. We just wanted them to wait. To go to college first. But they were young and headstrong, and so they eloped. We overreacted. Tempers flared on both sides. If only we could go back and do things differently. But of course we can't.

Joann Conrad sent me the picture of your fourth-grade reading club that was in the newspaper after you won the county contest. Chloe, you are the spitting image of your father! You were so little when he died, you probably don't remember much about him, but rest assured, he lives on in you. He had so many wonderful qualities, and I just know he's passed them on to you.

Hastily, I blot teardrops from the card with the sleeve of my pajamas. I don't want the ink to smear. I gaze at the photo of my parents for a long time, letting the love they had for each other, and later for me, engulf me.

I have just one memory of my father, and it's barely even a memory. More like an impression. We're outside in the summertime, at a beach or a pool. His face is above mine, but the sun is behind him, so I can't make out his features. All I can see is brightness and a glimmer of golden hair. Mostly I remember the way I felt. Safe. Loved. And oh so content.

I've heard about people who were resuscitated after their hearts stopped beating, and they all tell the same story. After they died, they went through a tunnel and at the end there was a bright light that was emanating pure love.

That's how I remember my father. As a brightness. As pure love.

Chapter 35

The mall story is in the news for weeks and turns everybody's thoughts to the bigger issue, the decline of the downtown area. A lot of people say that while they don't approve of what Ron Caldwell did, they can understand his desperation. An effort gets underway to bring downtown back to life, to turn it into a thriving business center. It's too late for Ron, of course, but the project will help lots of other people.

Jack Caldwell gets in trouble over the door locks that trapped my friends and me in the mall. He has to pay a hefty fine for violating safety code requirements and is ordered to redo the locks on all the mall doors so people can get out in an emergency, day or night.

I talk Ash into joining the poetry club. We become friends with Prisha and Carlie, and the four of us hang out regularly after school—at Ash's big, beautiful house or my humbler one, which has a mall conveniently attached to it. Prisha and Carlie and I counsel Ash about her home situation. On our advice, Ash asks her mom to talk to her dad about easing up. Ash's mom does something even better—she files for divorce.

Ash immediately drops all the lessons. With her dad out of the house, she becomes happier and more confident and stops tossing her head around in that haughty way that probably wasn't true haughtiness at all but just her way of keeping her self-esteem up, sort of like how the act of smiling is supposed to make you feel more cheerful. At least that's my mother's theory.

Ash starts inviting everybody to call her Ash. She's working hard to improve her image, and she thinks Ash sounds friendlier.

With more time to devote to her writing, she churns out some amazing poems. She's a much better poet than I'll ever be. Prisha and Carlie, look out. I think I can predict the winner of next year's poetry contest.

Kenny and Kevin announce that for the first time ever, they're going to go in different directions sports-wise. Kenny will be going out for springtime baseball, while Kevin is sticking with soccer. This gives me great hope for their futures.

I decide not to straighten my hair. I can finally see what everyone else saw all along—my hair is beautiful just the way it is. Plus, it's a connection with my father I never want to lose.

Mom is dating Good Cop, also known as Officer Drew Pritts. This is the first time she has dated since my dad died, which makes it a pretty big deal.

I always thought I'd be upset if my mom got a boyfriend, but I'm actually fine with it. Maybe the time is right, or maybe it's the guy who's right. Drew is kind through and through, and he never makes me feel like he's stealing my mother away. The bad news is, he's never had the slightest yearning to be a veterinarian, even though he loves animals. I guess I can live with that.

Drew is widowed like Mom and has a six-year-old daughter, Maddie, who is really sweet and who looks up to me like I'm some kind of teen idol. I've already started thinking of her as my little sister.

On the day Greetings got egged, Drew was the first police officer to arrive. He went through the mall, checking things out, and on a whim decided to make a wish on our chimney. He'd bought coffee at a convenience store that morning, and the change he got back included a fifty-cent piece. That was the coin he threw, because it was the only one big enough to accommodate his wish. What he wished for was a special lady to share his life with.

A short while later, he and my mother saw each other for the first time. Nothing happened that day except they noticed each other in a very singular way.

Fast-forward to the day of the bomb threat. When my mother was frantic because she just knew I was still in the mall even though Hal insisted otherwise, it was Drew who stayed with her and comforted her and promised to get to the bottom of things. And when Robby and the twins got out and reported that Ash and I were still inside, Drew led the way into the tunnel to find us. That was the day Mom realized there was finally room in her heart for a new man.

Mom says they're taking things slowly. Maybe they'll end up getting married, or maybe they won't. If they do, I know what I'm going to give them for a wedding present—that fifty-cent piece, mounted on top of a love poem and centered in a beautiful frame.

Mom finally reconciled with her parents. A few days after the bomb threat, I saw an envelope addressed to Doug and Laura Trimpey in our outgoing-mail pile. It was clearly a card, not a letter, and that disappointed me a little. But when you've been out of touch for so long, maybe it's easier to let a greeting card company do your talking at first.

Mom and I will be traveling to Tampa, Florida, next summer to spend a week with the Trimpeys. In the meantime, my grandparents and I have been getting to know each other through phone calls and e-mails and video chats, so when we visit, we won't feel like strangers.

The only mail Mom and I mark Return to Sender these days is from R. Caldwell, c/o West Virginia State Penitentiary. He'll be apologizing and explaining and excusing and begging for the rest of his life, but we don't want to hear it.

Chapter 36

On a slurping, gurgling, dripping day in March, my mother says we're going for a ride. But she won't tell me where.

"It's raining," I say when I catch my first glimpse of the great outdoors. "Couldn't we take this mystery trip some other day?"

The car is at the end of the parking lot, so far away we practically need binoculars to see it.

She hands me an umbrella. "Walk fast."

"Why won't you tell me where we're going?" I ask as we collapse our sodden umbrellas and hurl ourselves into the car.

"Because it's a surprise. I'll tell you this much—there's somebody special I want you to meet."

We drive for fifteen minutes. I don't pay attention to our route, because I'm busy exchanging text messages with Robby and Prisha. Mom got me a cell phone for Christmas because she wants me to always have a way to summon help in an emergency.

I look up when the car swings sharply to the right and comes to a stop. We're parked on a concrete driveway in front of a two-story red brick house. Another car sits next to ours in the driveway, facing the road. There's a lady inside with nicely styled blonde hair, and I assume she's the person Mom wants me to meet. But Mom doesn't even introduce us. She just winds down her window, and the lady, who's talking on her cell phone, mouths, "It's open."

"Come on," says Mom, getting out of the car.

The rain has diminished to a fine mist. We leave the umbrellas in the car.

"Well, here we are," says Mom as we walk up the driveway. She giggles like a nervous teenager. "Here's the somebody I wanted you to meet."

"Who?" I look around, mystified. "All I see is a house."

"Exactly!" A huge smile spreads across her face. "What do you think? Should we buy it?"

"Wh—what?" I'm so astounded, I choke on my own saliva. "Are you serious?"

"Serious as a bomb threat," she says lightly. "Three bedrooms, two bathrooms, a big back yard, and the price is right."

I grin incredulously.

She nods toward the house. "Shall we go in and take a look around?"

Things happen quickly after that. Mom makes an offer, and the owners accept it. We move in five weeks later. My bedroom window overlooks the back yard, which has a twittering forest behind it. I spend a lot of time sitting at my window, just drinking in all that nature—grass, trees, sky, bunnies, birds. Sometimes my new Persian kittens, Jolly and Jo-Jo, sit with me, purring like air purifiers as I scratch their silky heads.

On nice days I go exploring. Our road is a quiet one, and the houses are far enough apart that nobody feels crowded. I quickly discover that six kids from my school live within a quarter mile in either direction, and four more live a little bit beyond that. But I think my mother knew that when she picked this house.

As the days lengthen and temperatures rise, we kids move our leisure-time lives outdoors. We dam up the creek that winds through the woods. We build a tree house in Mark Larson's back yard. We begin to plan a summer carnival. On balmy nights we play flashlight tag.

At long last I'm part of a neighborhood, and it's just as great as I thought it would be.

In the new house, Mom and I stop separating bananas. That's mainly because of the banana holder Anna Hastings gave us as a housewarming gift. It's a shiny metal stand with a hook at the top that the bananas hang from, and it's supposed to help them ripen evenly. Mom and I are happy as can be that we no longer have to go hunting for bananas in strange places. And the bananas, I think, are happier too.

One night when I'm lying in bed listening to spring peepers through my open window and breathing in the moist nighttime air, a funny thought comes to me. The bananas in the strangest place of all were Mom and me! Because what could be stranger than living in a shopping mall? Just like our sock-drawer, toilet-tank, under-the-couch bananas, we were separated from our own kind, living lonely, isolated lives. People, like bananas, belong in a clump, I decide.

I think there might be a poem in that thought, and maybe someday I'll write it. For now, though, I'm too busy with other things.

Chapter 37

To no one's surprise, Jack Caldwell decides to tear down our house and fill the space with rent-generating kiosks. First, though, he figures he might as well cash in on all the bomb threat publicity by opening our house to the public. *"Tour the house that was occupied by the tragic Oasis Mall Family! Explore the secret tunnel used by the notorious mall vandal!"* The guided tour costs five dollars for people twelve and up, while younger kids are free.

Jack runs the tours for several months, until people lose interest. Then he sets the date for the demolition.

Mom and I are invited to attend. I don't want to go, but Mom thinks we should, "for closure."

On a sunny Sunday morning in June, we stand at the upper-level railing in the Farringer's wing with Jack Caldwell and a handful of other people. Below us several yellow construction vehicles operated by men in hardhats wheel around aimlessly, like giant beetles.

A foreman gives the signal, and the vehicles start bumping our house from various directions.

It doesn't take long before the old boards give out. The house gives a great shudder and falls in upon itself. It is dying as surely as my father died, and his father, and Connie. Grief swells in my throat and my vision gets blurry. Still I keep watching.

Soon the fireplace is the only thing standing, its

chimney reaching stubbornly toward the skylights. It gets clobbered by a wrecking ball and topples into the yard with a great crashing noise. Two workers begin jack-hammering the chimney into a pile of broken bricks while several others pile boards into tidy stacks.

We stand there for a long time, my mother and I, gazing down at the debris that was once our home.

A glint of silver catches my eye, and I watch as a single coin rolls away from the wreckage. It stops at the foot of a hard-hatted young woman, who picks it up and pockets it. I can't help noticing her T-shirt, which is yellow like my father's hair and reads "There's No Place Like Home."

I think about our little two-story house, the kids in my neighborhood, my friends at school, and the bananas hanging in a comfortable clump on the kitchen counter. And I smile.

"Hey," I say, tugging at my mother's arm. "Come on. Let's go home."

Writing a Book Review

Writing a book review can be fun! (And it's easier than you think.)

Thank you for reading *Mall Girl Meets the Shadow Vandal.* Did you like this book? If so, I hope you'll recommend it to friends, relatives, classmates, and anyone else who might enjoy it. In addition, please think about posting a book review on any of the websites where this book is sold or featured (Amazon, Barnes and Noble, Goodreads, Bookbub, etc.). If you've never posted a book review before, ask a parent or other grownup for help.

Book reviews help other readers decide which books might interest them. In addition, writing a review is a great way to practice your writing skills—plus it's exciting to see something you wrote featured on an Internet site. You'll also be doing the author a favor because authors *love* to get reviews. Posting a review is a win-win-win situation!

Writing a book review isn't like writing a book report for school. You don't have to summarize the whole story. Instead, just give your opinion about the book. Tell whether you liked or disliked it and explain why.

Are you ready to write a book review? Below are some questions to get you started. But you don't have to answer all of them. That would make for a very long review! Just pick a few things to write about.

First impressions

What made you want to read this book? Did a friend recommend it? Did you read about it on the Internet? Did you see it advertised in a magazine or catalog? Did you find it in a library?

Did the title capture your interest? Does it do a good job of summing up the story?

Do you like the cover? Do you think it fits the story?

Setting (where and when the story happened)

Did the author do a good job of describing the setting? Could you see the places in your mind?

Do you think the story would be better or worse if it happened in a different place or time?

Characters

Did the characters seem like real people? Did they remind you of anyone you know?

Who was your favorite character? What did you like about them?

Did you dislike any of the characters? If so, why?

Did you change your opinion of any characters over the course of the story? For instance, maybe you disliked a character at first but grew to like them as you learned more about them.

Was it easy to understand why each character acted the way they did?

Story (also known as plot)

Did the story hold your interest, or did you find parts of it boring?

How did the story make you feel—excited, scared, happy, sad, angry, or something else?

Did the plot keep you guessing, or was it easy to predict what would happen next?

Were there times when you could hardly wait to turn the page to find out what happened next?

Were there any confusing parts or questions that didn't get answered?

Did certain parts of the story make you laugh, cry, or gasp in surprise?

What was your favorite part of the story? What was your least favorite part?

If you had written this story, would you have done anything differently?

Author

Did this book make you want to read other books by the same author?

Your recommendations and rating

Would you recommend this book to other readers?

Are there certain kinds of readers you think would enjoy this story—for example pre-teens, younger readers, or fans of mystery stories?

How many stars would you give this book? Most sites let you rate a book by giving it one to five stars. One star means you hated the book. Five stars mean you loved it.

Tips for writing a review

Read reviews posted by other people to get ideas for writing your own review.

Pretend someone asked you if they should read the book. Write what you would tell them.

Give your review a title that sums up how you felt about the book—for instance, "Kept me guessing" or "So scary, I slept with the light on!" Avoid titles that don't say much, like "Really good story."

Try to write at least 100 words. That's about how many words are in this "Tips for writing a review" section.

Make sure you don't give away too much—especially the ending. Nobody likes spoilers!

A word about the author...

Kimberly Baer wrote her first story at age six. It was about a baby chick that hatched out of a little girl's Easter egg after somehow surviving the hard-boiling process. Nowadays she enjoys writing middle-grade and young adult fiction.

She lives in Virginia, where she likes to go power-walking on days when it's not too hot, too cold, too rainy, too snowy, or too windy. On indoor days, you might find her binge-watching one of her favorite TV shows: *Gilmore Girls*, *Friends*, or *The Office*.

You can call her "Kim." All her friends do.

Visit her at:

www.kimberlybaer.com

Thank you for purchasing
this publication of The Wild Rose Press, Inc.

For questions or more information
contact us at
info@thewildrosepress.com.

The Wild Rose Press, Inc.
www.thewildrosepress.com

CPSIA information can be obtained
at www.ICGtesting.com
Printed in the USA
LVHW081416230321
682225LV00031B/279

9 781509 235124